"Are we fighting or playing?"

Joe's husky voice had lost all trace of humor. Their rough breathing sounded abnormally loud.

And arousing.

"I...I don't know," Caitlin said, staring at Joe with her huge, glowing eyes. "I thought we were fighting. But now...I've lost track."

Joe had, too. His heart was pounding, his body responding to the tight, erotic hold he had on her. His mouth was only inches from hers. When her lips parted slightly he nearly groaned. "This is crazy," he muttered.

"Yeah. Insane." But she leaned closer and her soft breasts pressed into his chest.

He was lost.

"Stop me," he begged, nipping at the corner of her delicious mouth. "Stop me, Caitlin."

"I...don't think I want to stop you." She sounded breathless. *Confused. Aroused.*

"Hell. So we're both crazy." And with that, he kissed her.

Jill Shalvis is the award-winning, bestselling author of over a dozen romance novels. She's been making up stories to keep herself out of trouble since the day she learned to talk, and is very thankful to now get paid for doing what comes naturally.

The idea for *Who's the Boss?* has been playing out in her head for quite a while now, starting when her favorite boss fell in love with her ten years ago. Luckily she fell, too, and they're living happily ever after at Lake Tahoe with their three young children and far too many raccoons!

While this is Jill's first book for Harlequin Temptation, watch for more to come from this talented and prolific writer.

WHO'S THE BOSS?
Jill Shalvis

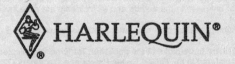

HARLEQUIN®

TORONTO • NEW YORK • LONDON
AMSTERDAM • PARIS • SYDNEY • HAMBURG
STOCKHOLM • ATHENS • TOKYO • MILAN • MADRID
PRAGUE • WARSAW • BUDAPEST • AUCKLAND

To good bosses everywhere, especially mine—
D. S. Builders.

You're the best.

ISBN 0-373-25842-9

WHO'S THE BOSS?

Copyright © 1999 by Jill Shalvis.

This edition published by arrangement with Harlequin Books S.A.

® and TM are trademarks of the publisher. Trademarks indicated with
® are registered in the United States Patent and Trademark Office, the
Canadian Trade Marks Office and in other countries.

Visit us at www.romance.net

Printed in U.S.A.

1

"A JOB," CAITLIN TAYLOR muttered for the hundredth time. She paused from straightening her silk stockings to roll her eyes upward with a wry grimace. "I hope you and God are having a good laugh, Dad. You certainly got the last one on me."

Her heart ached as it had all month, ever since her father had unexpectedly passed away from kidney failure.

It might have hurt a little less, she admitted, if he hadn't given away his fortune to everyone but his own daughter. Instead, he'd left her...a job.

At least he'd done that. In her ice-blue satin lingerie, she faced the full-length mirror. Her reflection wavered as fear gripped her, but she had no illusions. Her naturally wavy blond bob, no matter how she combed it, made her look as if she'd just climbed out of bed. Her overly curvaceous body refused to be tamed by exercise. This morning, her deep brown eyes were heavy from lack of sleep, and already carefully accented with liner and mascara. She looked like a young, beautiful woman with the world at her fingertips.

If only it were true.

Caitlin gave a half laugh and shoved back the unaccustomed fear and panic.

She'd never held a job in her life. Her father had spoiled his only child. In all her twenty-four years, she had only a handful of memories of him, mostly due to his heavy traveling and prominent social schedule. Still, as her only family, he'd made sure her every material need had been met. Fashion had been her first love, and he'd given in to it. Milan, Paris, New York, Los Angeles…she knew these places intimately; they were her playgrounds. She'd gone to designing school in Paris and New York, both on her father's bank account, but the truth was, she wasn't talented enough to make it in that cutthroat world. Since then she hadn't been idle— far from it, for organizing society events was a particular talent of hers, even if it didn't count as a job, or earn her money.

Her father had kept her in style, making sure she had a healthy monthly allowance deposited directly into her account.

That had stopped abruptly with his death, and grief had been forced to take a back seat to survival.

With every credit card her father had ever given her maxed out, less than one month's rent in her bank account and no more allowance, Caitlin faced serious trouble. Enough trouble, she'd finally admitted to herself, that she'd have to swallow her pride and take the poor-paying job she'd been left in her father's will.

"A clerical position," Caitlin said with another humorless laugh that didn't quite cover up her confusion and pain. "And me not knowing the difference between a fax machine and a scanner."

She walked to her brimming wall-length closet and sighed, knowing that by this time next month she would be living in some dismal little apartment. Bye-bye southern-California beachfront condo. Again, her heart leaped at the betrayal of her father's abrupt desertion. *Why?* she wondered frantically. Why would her father indulge and spoil her all her life, then desert her this way? She didn't understand, but wallowing was getting her nowhere.

With effort, she shrugged into the devil-may-care persona she showed the world. What did one wear for a job that required an eight-o'clock showing? But while she dressed, her thoughts continually drifted back to the burning questions—why had her father pawned her off on some little subsidiary of what had once been a huge engineering conglomerate? A conglomerate split up by his will, all the pieces going to different investors who'd been his close friends.

Friends had rated higher than his own daughter.

Now Caitlin was slated to work for some pencil-laden, calculator-carrying engineer nerd named Joseph Brownley. Because he'd worked with her father for years, she imagined him as old, crusty, tough. Mean.

Shuddering, she slipped into what she hoped looked businesslike enough—a short red crepe de chine suit. The pumps she added gave her an extra three and a half inches, *and* some badly needed self-confidence. She wanted to look sophisticated. Polished. But while she seemed to be able to fool everyone else, she couldn't pull the wool over her own eyes. She looked flighty, ditzy and wild, which sent her back to the bathroom in another attempt to tame her hair with ruthless brush strokes and styling spritz.

She could do this. But for one weak moment, she sank to the bed. Could she? Could she do anything but organize parties for the rich and famous? And how hard would it really be to charge for those services?

Hard, she admitted.

So hard she'd rather do this...work in an office.

But could she really survive on her own?

Swallowing back a sudden sob, Caitlin lifted her chin and forced a bright smile. Her knees trembled as she stood, but she stiffened them and lifted her chin. She had no place in her life for pathetic self-pity or fear, only determination.

The outfit didn't work.

Too showy, she decided with a hasty glance at her slim gold watch. She ripped off the suit to try again, tossing it carelessly aside. No telling what Mr. Brownley thought of tardiness, but if he fired her before she'd even started, she'd really be in trouble. And with her only true working talent being that she could navigate the mazed streets of any garment district blindfolded, who else in his right mind would hire her?

Coming to yet another abrupt halt in front of her mirror, she took a tough, no-holds-barred look at herself. Snug, cropped frost-blue sweater over a long, flowing flowery skirt. Heels, of course—she never went anywhere without heels. But too casual, darn it! She added a muted linen jacket and hoped for the best. As she ran to her car, huffing and puffing from the exertion of the morning, she grumbled about the unearthly hour.

God, she hated mornings.

She thrust her little BMW into gear, leaving her exclusive Newport Beach neighborhood hours before she normally even stirred from her bed. As she hit the packed 405 freeway, she realized her first mistake in allowing only thirty minutes to get from the beach to downtown Irvine. It seemed the entire population of southern California started work at the same time, and given that she was cut off three times before she even hit the first on-ramp, apparently everyone was just as irritable and late as she.

At the interchange, no one would let her over. Frustrated, she tried one of her flirtatious winks and got…a very rude hand gesture.

Did normal people do this every day?

The thought made her shudder. Yes, she was sheltered, but she had friends who worked. *No, she didn't*, she reminded herself. Hadn't she learned that in the past few weeks, as one by one, her so-called friends had ditched her when the terms of her father's will became public?

She was alone, truly alone, for the first time in her entire existence.

And she was going to be very late. No big surprise, of course. Her father had always claimed she'd be late for her own funeral. She'd certainly been late for his, but that had been because the limo she'd counted on all her life had vanished. Repossessed. By the time she'd driven herself, she'd missed the entire service. She knew her father wouldn't have been surprised, but she had a feeling being late *today* was a luxury she couldn't afford.

This little bubble of stress sitting uncomfortably in her belly was new and entirely unwelcome. So was the apprehension about her future, and the lingering, gnawing wound of her father turning his back on her.

She came to a grinding halt in the fast lane, surrounded by thousands of other idling cars. Never one to obsess about anything, she couldn't believe she'd been doing just that all morning.

Shaking her head, she cranked up the music, sat back to wait out the traffic and cleared her mind.

JOE'S FINGERS FLEW over the keyboard. Deep in concentration, he'd been working for hours, but he couldn't stop now. He was so close, so very close, to getting it right.

"Joe."

Vaguely, he heard a female voice calling him, and just as vaguely, he knew it was Darla.

He ignored her.

All those years, he'd had to work on hardware, designing computers for his bread and butter...but no more. Now, with Edmund Taylor's generosity in death—Joe's heart squeezed at the reminder—he could work on his first love. *Software.* And he was inches away from perfecting the system he envisioned revolutionizing every office in the country.

"Joe."

Just another few minutes, he thought, stretching cramped legs that were far too long to be shoved beneath a desk for so many hours. A few more minutes and things might click into place. He could almost hear the big software companies knocking at his door. *Bill Gates, eat your heart out.*

"Joe? Yoo-hoo..."

Without taking his eyes off the keyboard, he growled, waving one hand wildly over his shoulder, his usual sign for *Leave me the hell alone!* With the ease only the hyperfocused can achieve, he sank back into his thoughts. *Just put that command here instead of over there—*

"I'm sorry, Joe."

"No problem," he murmured automatically, not looking up. Why had he chosen to work in the front office, instead of his own down the hall, which would have given him more privacy?

Because he'd been in a rush, that's why. Always in a rush. "Go away."

"*Joe*," said a now laughing Darla. "Could you *please* look at me?"

With a sigh, he straightened, biting back his impatience. He shoved his fingers through already unruly hair and took his gaze off the screen long enough to glare at the only person who would dare interrupt him. "What? What do you want?"

Darla smiled sweetly. "Lovely to see you, too."

"Great. Nice. Now go away." He'd already turned back to the computer when she spoke again.

"Joe, could you focus those baby blues this way for just another minute? Pretty please?"

"I'm really busy," he said evenly, through his teeth. His fingers itched to get back to the keyboard.

"But—"

"*This*," he announced, "is why I need an assistant. To keep people out."

"You couldn't *keep* an assistant," Darla told him, gesturing to the cluttered office, which admittedly looked as though World War III had gone off in it. Papers were everywhere. So were books, files and an entire city of computer parts. "No one but those other crazy computer programmers you've got back there wants to work for a perfectionist, a workaholic, a technical—"

"*Why* are you here? Just tell me that much," he begged, resting his fingers on the keyboard and eyeing the screen longingly.

"Oh, wipe that frown off your pretty face— I'm not here to bug you for your tax info. Yet."

Darla's insulted scowl worked, and Joe laughed. As the only accountant in their small building, the tall, waiflike Italian beauty had taken on all of the other four businesses in the place, his included. Besides handling most of their bookkeeping, she dished out unwanted advice, unsolicited sisterly affection and more than a few good dirty jokes. "And what could be more important than tax stuff?" he teased, and resigned himself to a break.

"Not much." She grinned, too, making her look much younger than her thirty years. "But remember that assistant you were just mentioning? I think she's arrived. I saw her roaming around downstairs, scrutinizing the different suites and the business names on the front board as if she had no idea where she's going."

"I didn't hire an assistant."

"You told me Edmund wrote off his investment in this company, making it effectively yours—as long as you guaranteed his pathetically spoiled daughter a job."

"Yeah." Joe rubbed his hand over his chest at the twist of pain. Edmund, gone. Forever.

At the thought of Edmund's daughter, whom he'd never met, his usually receptive heart hardened. "She never even bothered to show up for her own father's funeral." He tried to remember what Edmund had told him about her. A flightly clotheshorse. A party girl. A world traveler—on her daddy's budget, of course.

Nothing particularly flattering.

"Whoever you saw couldn't be her," he stated. "A software company that has yet to prove itself has nothing to offer a socialite."

Darla shrugged. "Maybe not. But Marilyn Monroe's here." She sniffed and gave him a haughty glance that he had no trouble deciphering.

Joe wasn't ashamed to admit he'd had more than his fair share of women flit in and out of his life, and his good friend Darla had hated most of them. But nothing got her goat more than a blond bombshell. "She looks like Marilyn Monroe?" he asked, unable to contain his wide grin when Darla rolled her eyes. "Really?"

"Barbie meets *Baywatch*, actually," she snapped, making him laugh. Darla snorted in disgust. "What is it about that blond, wide-eyed, come-hither look that renders a man so stupid?"

"Ahh…a come-hither look?"

She glowered and straightened, her considerable height accentuating her thinness. "And she's got huge—"

"Darla," he said, still grinning as he cut her off. "She's *not* looking for me—she couldn't be. No way would Edmund's daughter show up." He hadn't read all of Edmund's book-length will, hadn't been able to bring himself to even open the five-inch-thick file that had been sent to him by Edmund's attorney, but he imagined Caitlin Taylor had gotten a very nice chunk of change. She'd have no need for a job.

He glanced at his watch. "And anyway, it's ten o'clock. What kind of an assistant would start work this late?" He happily gave his computer his full attention. "Now go away and let me be."

"Okay…but you asked for it."

Breathing a sigh of relief when she was gone, Joe looked at his screen with anticipation. Now he'd get some work done.

He'd simply kill the next person who interrupted him, he decided, and promptly forgot about everything except what he was doing.

In the back of his mind whirled the vision of his program up and running. And for once, thanks to Edmund, that dream was obtainable.

"Ahem."

Not again! He needed a weapon. Yeah, that was it. A squirt gun, maybe, or a—

"Excuse me."

"If the place isn't burning down," he growled, "then I don't—" Out of the corner of his eye, he saw her; words vanished from his brain. She was petite, luscious and one of the most beautiful women he'd ever seen. She smiled and his tongue actually went dry.

"Hi," she said, wiggling her fingers at him.

Trailing behind her, gawking with their collective mouths hanging open, were Vince, Andy and Tim, his three techs. At the moment, they resembled Larry, Curly and Moe. He sent them looks loaded with daggers, and they slunk back, closing the door behind him.

"I'm looking for Mr. Brownley," the exotic creature said in a sweet, musical voice. "I'm Caitlin Taylor."

Caitlin Taylor. Professional socialite. Ditzy, spoiled princess...*his new assistant.*

An imaginary noose settled around his neck. He liked gorgeous women as much as the next guy—maybe even more—but no way could he work with one, especially one with the life-style and attitude this one was reputed to have. He couldn't respect someone who didn't know what tough work meant, or the value of a hard-earned dollar, and Joe never worked with anyone he didn't one hundred percent respect. Never.

"This is CompuSoft, Inc., isn't it?" Her voice could arouse the dead, and Joe wasn't, unfortunately, dead. "I checked the suite number downstairs," she said. "You must be the receptionist."

He groaned inwardly and stood up from the front desk. *Never again,* he promised himself.

He'd work from the seclusion of his own office from now on.

She flashed another dazzling smile, leveling him with a pair of warm, dreamy brown eyes so deep he felt like swimming. "My father—"

Shit. Her father. His own mentor, beloved friend, father figure. Edmund Taylor had meant everything to him, and Joe had made him a promise. The noose tightened. "Your father told me about you," he managed to say around the month-old lump in his throat.

"He did?" She seemed surprised. "So you know I'll be working here?"

Joe nodded, wondering what to do. He'd never broken a promise and he didn't want to start now, especially not when it came to Edmund, but he had absolutely no use for this woman in his company. None at all.

"Maybe you can tell me something about this place. About the boss," she added with another sweet smile as she moved gracefully into the room. Her skirt flowed around her ankles, clung to her thighs. The light blazer she wore parted in the middle, revealing her sweater, snugged tight over her soft, perfect curves.

In any other situation, Joe knew he'd be flashing his most charming smile and already be deeply into flirt mode. This sort of woman was made for seduction, and while he didn't want to employ one, he loved the interplay.

But playing with her would be pleasure, and this was serious business. *His* business. His pride and joy. Dread filled him at the thought. With this woman around, none of the guys, all of whom drooled at anything in a skirt, would get an ounce of productive work done.

"Is he nice?" she wondered with a slight frown. "Patient?"

"Who?"

A little laugh escaped her. "The boss, silly. You know, Mr. Brownley."

"Uh...nice? No," he said decisively, standing. The top of her head didn't quite meet his chin. She was petite, feminine, beautiful. And he didn't want her here. "He's really...awful. Hard to work for. *Ugly*," he added desperately.

Caitlin's brow puckered as she considered this. "That really doesn't have anything to do with—"

"You should leave. Now." The idea sprouted from nowhere. He wouldn't be breaking his promise if she left, right? It wouldn't be his fault. "You should go before he sees you."

Caitlin cocked her head to one side and studied him sympathetically. "He makes you nervous, doesn't he?" She inhaled deeply, drawing his attention downward. Dangerously downward, causing his hormones to do a quick, instinctive dance.

"Don't worry," she told him with a confidence he could see was more bravado than anything else. "Maybe now that he has me to help him, he'll be nicer."

Guilt stabbed him. "Uh...yes...well..."

"Things will work out," she soothed, her face open and clear of anything but genuine emotion, which only deepened his guilt. "You'll see. I'll fawn over him a bit. You know, mother him."

Joe had never been mothered, and maybe because of that he tended to have a low opinion of anyone who relied heavily on those family-type affections. "That probably won't help much," he admitted.

"Everyone needs mothering."

"Not everyone." Not Joseph Brownley. He didn't need anyone. Period. Never would. But she seemed so optimistic, while at the same time so touchingly full of nerves, that he lost his desire to continue the farce, even if she were just a gorgeous piece of fluff. "Look—"

"It's all right," she said gently, nodding her head. Wild blond hair flew around her face, cupping her rosy cheeks, framing huge eyes that were surprisingly sharp and self-aware. "I'll be fine."

"No, you don't understand—"

"Yes, I do. You're trying to be kind."

Kind. Joe might have laughed. He'd certainly never been accused of kindness before. "No," he assured her with a tight smile. "I'm not."

"You don't have to tell me how bad of a monster he is." She swallowed hard, making Joe feel like a first-class jerk. "I really can handle it. Just...point me in the right direction." Her voice was a whisper now. "And I'll find out for myself."

Hell. "You already have." Apology softened his voice, and he sighed with regret.

"What do you mean?"

Oh, he was going to have to face this, whether he wanted to or not, but on the other hand, so was she. This was no place for her, and the sooner she realized it, the better for the both of them. "I mean you probably should have left while you had the chance."

Her eyes reflected her confusion, and he didn't blame her. "I'm the monster," he said. "Joe Brownley."

2

"*You're Joe Brownley?*" Caitlin tripped over her tongue, but she couldn't help it.

She was shocked, to say the least.

"I'm afraid so."

"But..." Good Lord. Well over six feet of rangy, powerful male stared back at her. His ice-blue eyes narrowed, cloudy with thoughts he hid with ease. Although with that square, unforgiving jawline, she could guess he wasn't especially thrilled. His sun-tipped light brown hair curled carelessly over his collar, as if he couldn't be bothered with it. Wide, huge hands rested on his hips, his feet placed firmly apart. He looked utterly poised and self-assured. He wore a plain white T-shirt that bulged over impressive biceps, and faded, snug jeans that fit the man all too well.

He looked like a ruffian. A hood. A gorgeous, *temperamental* hood.

What happened to her old, pencil-laden, calculator-carrying geek? This man was young—early thirties at the most—sharp and, judging by his scowl, tough as nails.

At first he'd seemed sweet and friendly, but no longer. Now he was the complete opposite.

And to think she'd been worried about _him_, and his fear of the wrath of the "boss"!

"Oh, dear," she whispered. "This isn't going to work out at all."

Relief flooded his features, softening them. "Really?"

An audible groan came from the other side of the wall. In a flash, Joseph's scowl was back. He reached around her with one long arm and yanked open the door. Three guys—at least two of whom fit her computer-geek image to the last microinch—nearly fell into the room.

They recovered quickly, especially with the glare they received from Joe, and mumbling assorted apologies, slunk back down the hallway.

"Sorry," Joe told Caitlin. "We're short on excitement around here. You were saying this wasn't going to work out?"

She nodded, wondering how a computer nerd could possibly have such a low, husky voice, like fine-aged whiskey. "Yes. I'm sorry. But…well, in my experience, I don't work well with men like you."

He blinked. _"Men like me?"_

A sound came from behind the once again shut door. It sounded like a…snicker. Three snickers.

Joe inhaled deeply and ignored them.

Caitlin pictured the three men once again pressed against the closed door, listening with their ears glued to the wood. She might have smiled, were it not for the frown on Joseph's face.

"What's that supposed to mean?" he wanted to know, straightening his wide shoulders. "That you don't work well with men like me?"

It meant that she was tired of pushing away roaming hands and groping fingers from the kind of man who took her at face value. Tired of being patted on the head as if she were a toy, a pretty, empty shell of a human being.

It had been happening to her ever since puberty, which had come unfortunately early. In her experience, the kind of man most likely to treat her that way stood right in front of her. Cool, collected, knowing, cocky.

"It simply means I'm sorry, Mr. Brownley," she said. "But this won't work out at all. It's clear that you're a man who needs no one. Certainly not me." Caitlin turned, got to the door before she remembered something horrifying.

She needed this job desperately.

Without it, she was headed for the poorhouse. It'd been so easy for her to forget that little detail, being a woman completely unused to stress.

Could she find another job?

The idea almost made her laugh. With her qualifications, she'd be lucky to land the front-counter job at Del Taco. Her hand stilled on the doorknob, and she grappled with pride and fear and something even newer...annoyance.

Why hadn't he wanted her?

"Did you forget where you parked your car?" Joe inquired politely from behind her.

Great. The sexy thug was a smartass to boot. "No." Plastering her friendliest smile in place, Caitlin turned back to face the sternest-looking cute guy she'd ever seen. "I just thought that maybe..." Oh, how she hated to eat crow. "Maybe I judged you too quickly."

He stared at her for a long moment, his cool eyes giving nothing of himself away. They both ignored the multiple sharp intakes of breath from the other side of the door. "Does this mean you're *not* leaving?" he asked finally.

She winced at the unmistakable regret in his tone. "That's what it means," she admitted. "Unless I'm fired."

"From what I know of you, you have absolutely no experience in much of anything, except maybe *social* studies."

She stiffened in automatic defense at the disapproval and disgust. "I can do this job."

He sighed heavily. "Dammit. I can't fire you anyway. It's complicated."

From the other side of the door came a joint sigh of relief that made her feel marginally better. At least his employees wanted her to stay. She relaxed marginally with relief. She hadn't failed yet!

I'll show you, Dad. I can do this. But then his words sank in. "You can't fire me? How come?"

His already impossibly hard jaw hardened

even more. "Never mind. What do you know about being a secretary?"

"Uh…" What she knew would fit in her back pocket—if she had one. "I can make coffee," she improvised, drawing on the one skill she thought she probably shared with every good secretary.

Joe Brownley closed his eyes and groaned.

"And," she added brilliantly, completely undeterred by his response, "I have a really nice telephone voice!"

Joe was first and foremost a thinker. There was nothing he liked less than to not understand something—and he didn't come close to understanding Edmund's daughter. "Tell me this," he begged. "*Why* do you want this job?"

"Well…that's a long story." A shrug lifted her petite shoulders *and* her not so petite breasts, which were already straining against her sweater. "I doubt you'd understand."

"I'm of average intelligence," he said dryly. "Try me."

Curious now, he crossed his arms and leaned back against the door frame. "You're rich as sin, princess. And I know for a fact your father had you in a beachfront condo, and a fancy car."

She laughed shortly, her doe eyes looking a little wild.

"So why do you want a job like this?"

"I just do." She licked her lips. "And the will says you'll give it to me."

She was right, and the reminder of it was a

slap in the face. Edmund had given Joe everything, *everything*, and in return he'd asked for
only one little favor.

It was time to stop griping about it and accept
the facts. For better or worse, he was stuck with
his new assistant.

At least until she quit.

"Okay, Ms. Taylor," he said wearily, rubbing
his temples. "Here's how this is going to work.
I'm in the middle of something pretty important
and hate to be bothered. I guess I could use
someone to handle the phones."

A cheer went up on the other side of the door;
Joe hauled it open. Again, the three young men
stumbled awkwardly into the room. Immediately, they all straightened, tried to look casual.

Disgusted, Joe said, "These yo-yos are my
techs," he told Caitlin. "Huey, Dewey and
Louie."

Two of them were identical twins. One of the
tall, skinny, dark-haired twenty-odd-year-olds
stuck out his hand, a wide grin on his face. "Hi.
I'm Andy." He pumped Caitlin's hand so enthu-
siastically, she feared he might pull her arm
right out of the socket, but his expression was so
kind, so sincere, she just smiled back, relieved
beyond speech by the friendly face.

"I provide tech support to our customers," he
said. "As well as keeping Joe here human by
dragging him out of here every night."

Human? Could have fooled her.

"I'm Tim," said the other twin. He, too,

grinned from ear to ear. "I also help with tech support, but basically Joe couldn't function without me because I have all the charm and personality."

Joe rolled his eyes.

Tim nodded. "It's true." He looked at Caitlin, his eyes shining with good humor. "And you're really great."

"Thank you," said Caitlin smiling, thinking they were pretty great, too.

The third, a medium-built redhead who looked to be in his early thirties, smiled shyly and kept his hands firmly in his pockets when he introduced himself. "I'm Vince. I work in product development with Joe."

"We've been wanting a new secretary," Tim said into the awkward silence. "Really bad. Ever since the last one…uh…left."

Andy nodded emphatically. "Joe scared her off, and—" He broke off at the look on Joseph's face.

Another awkward silence. Tim bit his lip. Andy stared at his feet. Vince watched Caitlin send a curious, cautious glance to Joe. "She, uh…didn't work out," Vince said diplomatically. "It wasn't really anyone's fault exactly."

Joe scoffed. "No need to mince words, Vince. You can tell her the truth."

Whether it was loyalty or simple resistance to Joseph's tone, Vince remained silent, stubbornly buttoning his lip.

"I'll tell her," Tim piped up in a stage whisper

that everyone within three miles could have heard. He looked at Caitlin and confided, "Joe scared the last three women off. You don't scare easily, do you?"

"I…" She thought of her bills. Of the creditors. "No."

"Joe's not all that great with women," Tim said.

Vince laughed softly when Joe shook his head, disgusted.

"We begged him to get someone in here to do the filing and answer the phones. And to lighten things up a bit. You know—someone to have fun with. That's all. No offense, you understand," Andy said quickly.

"None taken," Caitlin assured him, delighted with her sweet new workmates.

"But the longest any of them lasted is about three hours," admitted Tim.

Looking into the frowning, incredibly handsome face of Joe Brownley, Caitlin had no problem imagining why. "You don't say."

Vince laughed again, and some of the tension dispersed. "He's all bark, no bite," he assured her, but some of his amusement faded when Joe glared at him.

"Why is everyone talking about me as if I'm not standing right here?"

Vince ignored him. "Sort of like a terrier," he elaborated. "Loud and gruff. Then passive as a kitten."

"Really?" She eyed the very annoyed Joe. The

long, lean lines of his body were stiff. His eyes like ice. *Passive* was the *last* word she would have used.

"Back to work, guys," he said stiffly, his wide shoulders tense.

Tim hesitated at the door. "Nice to meet you, Caitlin. I hope you stay."

"Do you really know how to make coffee?" Andy asked plaintively. "Because—"

"Andy," Joe said, his voice careful and quiet. "Don't you have something, *anything*, to do?"

"Yeah, I guess." His shoulders slumped. "It's just that you make really crappy coffee, Joe. And—"

"I'm sure we'll have plenty of time to discuss the damn coffee," Joe grated out, clearly beyond patience. "I'd really, really like to get to work some time today. Would that be all right with everyone here?"

Vince leaned close to Caitlin, confiding, "He's only a bear because he's so close to finishing this project and all this other stuff keeps interrupting him. Phones, paperwork, stuff like that." He flashed a sweet smile. "Don't let him scare you off now, okay?"

He was so kind. So were the twins.

She couldn't remember if or when she'd been shown such simple, untethered friendship. Any friends she'd thought she had were gone. Vanished into thin air because she was no longer a somebody.

But these guys... They'd all looked her in the

eyes instead of her chest—another plus in their favor—when they'd talked to her, and while it was obvious they thought she was pretty, they'd treated her with respect.

Caitlin smiled, embarrassed to feel her throat tighten up at reliving their warm, eager greeting. She'd never in her life felt so welcome—the still scowling Joseph Brownley excluded—and a realization hit hard. Everywhere she'd gone, everything she'd done, she'd either been accepted for her looks or for her father's money.

Never for herself alone.

Everyone left and she was standing here with her boss. She knew darn well *he* didn't want her, that he didn't think she could handle this job. But for some reason, he wasn't going to refuse her.

He caught her gaze with his, and his jaw went all hard again. Most of her resolve wavered and what little there was left took a bad beating at his next words.

"Okay, princess, here's how this situation is going to work."

Where had that nice man gone? The one she'd first spoken with, the one she'd thought was going to be her friend? She looked carefully, but couldn't see a trace of him. It was almost as if once he had realized he was stuck with her, he'd purposely turned himself into someone she wouldn't like.

Well, he'd been partially successful, she

thought. She *didn't* like him, but she wouldn't run off because of it.

"Last door on the left is my office," Joe said gruffly, stepping into the hallway to point it out. "I hate to be interrupted, so stay out." He looked at her expectantly then, a little hopefully. Maybe she'd still run off if he were boorish enough?

As if she'd read his mind, she laughed at him. *Laughed.* The unexpected sweet sound had Joseph's stomach muscles tensing.

"Are you waiting for me to cower from such a fierce command?" She shook her head, her short blond bob flying. Her flowery fragrance wafted up, assaulting his nostrils, annoying him because she smelled so damn good he found himself straining for another sniff. "Or maybe, better yet, you think I'll run off with my tail between my legs."

Her words put a vivid picture in his mind of what *was* between her legs.

"Should I remind you whose daughter I am?" she asked, breaking into his startling sensual thoughts.

Her father had backed down to no one. "I know whose daughter you are."

"Good. And I don't frighten easily."

Mad at her, at his techs and at himself, he stalked back into the front office.

"Clearly," she muttered, "I'm to follow you."

Why today? he wondered helplessly. Why, when he was so damn close to finishing his program, did he have to deal with this? With a quick glance upward, he grimaced. *Thanks, Edmund. Hope you're getting a kick out of this.*

Caitlin passed him in the hallway. "Maybe I *would* be better off at Del Taco."

He watched as she sashayed prettily into the main office, her hips swinging in tune to his undisciplined hormones. "I'll give you a lift to the nearest one." Then, to soften the words he realized were unkind, he offered the sweetest smile he could.

She shook her head. "Well, I walked right into that one, didn't I?"

Her mouth was pouty, lusciously red, and the most inane thought popped into his head.

She must taste like heaven.

The woman was a blond bombshell, with a complete lack of work ethic, designed to torture him. And yet he couldn't stop thinking about what she'd look like spread across his desk wearing one of those come-hither looks.

"So...how many employees do you have here?" she wondered aloud, interrupting his erotically charged thoughts.

"Besides the three idiots you've already met, just me."

"And now me," Caitlin added.

"I'm doing my best to change that."

Ah, sarcasm. Well, she could understand that. The way he kept his big body so tense, she imagined he was quite uncomfortable. Most men, in her experience, fought unease with a sort of bearish aggression. Her father had been the king of that act, though he'd never used it on her, and she imagined this Mr. Brownley wasn't much different. "I'm sticking, Mr. Brownley."

"So you've said."

Her bravado was quickly taking a beating in the face of his stubbornness. Before she caved in completely, she tried small talk. "I thought CompuSoft was huge. According to my father, this place was the future of progressive software."

Incredibly, Joseph's eyes softened. His attitude vanished. "He said that?"

It was obviously an illusion that he suddenly appeared so vulnerable. He was about as vulnerable as a starving black bear waking from hibernation. "He was quite proud of this place."

His throat worked. His voice sounded hushed, almost reverent. "I take that as a huge compliment."

Her father never complimented lightly, and just thinking about him hurt when she was tired of hurting. He'd rarely complimented *her*. To combat the thought, she desperately continued her one-sided conversation. "How could you have only the four of you here?"

"This is no longer the huge corporation it was under your father. We've been siphoned off, separated from all his other various businesses. We're on our own, just a few of us designing and supporting software." He gave her that impenetrable stare again. "You didn't get a copy of the will?"

Caitlin noticed that whenever he mentioned her father, he watched her carefully. But she could hear his thick disapproval, and her stomach tightened in response to the unfamiliar stress purling through her.

If he only knew how she'd pored over that darn will, wondering what had happened to her nice, cozy life.

If only he had a clue as to how lost she felt in this new, unsafe world, or how much resentment for her father she harbored deep down in her heart.

"Yes," she managed to answer with her usual cheekiness, refusing to let him get to her. "I got it."

"If the terms were too difficult to comprehend," he said slowly, finally succeeding in stirring her rare temper, "you should have asked someone to explain it to you."

"Contrary to what you must believe about me, I do understand the written word."

"*All* of your father's companies were divested. CompuSoft was half-mine to start with, so he simply willed me the other half."

Her father could give this man half a company, just hand it over, and he couldn't leave her a penny. Couldn't leave her anything but a measly job with a man who couldn't abide her. It took every ounce of common courtesy she had not to resent Joe Brownley for this.

Well, okay, that was a big fat lie. She *did* resent him. A lot. "Nice of him."

"Nice?" He missed the sarcasm and let out a short laugh that seemed harsh. "It was incredible. The most generous thing anyone's ever done for me—" He stopped abruptly, stared at her. "I have no idea why I'm telling you this."

She didn't, either. It hurt unbelievably to know her father had thought so little of his own flesh and blood that he'd left this man more than he had his only child. "Where do I start?"

"So you're staying, then?"

"Yes."

He sighed. "Fine. This is the reception desk." He gestured behind him to a wide desk facing the entrance. At least, she assumed it was a desk; all she could see were stacks and stacks of paperwork, files, various computer parts and what looked like an old, forgotten take-out food bag.

"All you have to do is come in on time, which around here is eight o'clock, and answer the occasional phone." He sent her a long look. "Can you do that?"

"Hmm. I think I can manage." She was really going to have to teach him a thing or two about manners. As for the ungodly hour, she'd have to work on it. "Surely you have more needs than just answering your phone."

His light eyes darkened. His mouth curved, making her blink in surprise. Sullen, the man had been beyond handsome. Smiling, he was stunningly gorgeous.

"I don't think you want to hear about my needs."

No. No, she didn't, Caitlin decided as her heart took off running. "Probably not."

Slowly, he ran his gaze down the length of her, then back up. When he met her eyes with his, an unmistakable heat radiated from them. Caitlin had been on the receiving end of looks like that ever since she'd grown breasts, so she'd long ago learned to tune them out. Yet now, under Joe Brownley's suddenly hot gaze, as unbelievable as it seemed, she felt herself blush. "Something wrong with my attire?"

"Yeah," he said in that low, disturbingly sexy voice. "In this office, you'll need something a little…more."

She'd known it! Her clothes were all wrong. "More?"

"Shapeless. Like a potato sack."

She laughed. "I wouldn't be caught dead in a potato sack."

"You're distracting."

"Your techs were refreshing and charming. I don't think I'll have a problem here with them."

He turned and started back down the hall, his long legs churning up the distance in just a few strides. "I wasn't talking about the Three Stooges, princess," he called back.

Oh.

Oh.

3

THE BUILDING THAT HOUSED CompuSoft was small for downtown, Caitlin thought. But it was brick and glass and strangely cozy.

There was a small coffee stand on the lobby floor, complete with doughnuts, croissants and mouth-watering pastries. Caitlin couldn't resist stopping there before getting on the elevator, if only to drool.

After all, if she had to suffer mornings, then she needed junk food.

A lovely brunette woman, about Caitlin's age, wearing an apron and a harassed smile came up to her. "Can I help you?"

Caitlin thought of her last dollar drowning in the bottom of her purse. "How much is that chocolate thingie over there, last one on the row?"

"In calories or cents?"

Caitlin laughed. "Either way, I'm sure it's too expensive. Besides, I shouldn't. Oh, man, I really shouldn't." Ruefully, she tapped her curvy hips.

The woman let out a reluctant smile, which softened her entire face. Her green eyes sparkled with life that hadn't been there before. "This is what I tell myself every morning."

Caitlin eyed her spectacular figure—all willowy and slim. "How many do you eat?" she asked doubtfully.

She shrugged. "Depends on how rude the customers are, which varies. The more annoying jerks I serve, the more I eat."

Caitlin sighed and thought of Joe. "I'm afraid if I stopped here every time my boss annoyed me, I'd be busting out of my clothes in a week."

The woman laughed now, and gave Caitlin a much more genuine smile. "You're new here. I'm Amy."

"I'm Caitlin." She dug into her purse to appease her rumbling stomach, and accepted the huge chocolate pastry.

Amy grinned, removed her apron and grabbed a pastry for herself. "Just in case the crowd gets crazy later, I'll take my break now."

They pigged out together.

BY THE TIME HE GOT to his office the next morning, Joe was high on adrenaline, his mind racing ahead, thinking about his software program.

With a little luck, he figured he could make real headway today, if he got in the good ten to twelve hours he needed.

As previously arranged, he had first stopped at one of the local banks to meet with a loan officer, hoping to start the preapproval process. He wanted to be prepared when his program was complete, so he could properly promote and sell it. To do that, he'd need money—a lot of it.

Despite the hassles ahead, he grinned and silently thanked Edmund for the thousandth time. Without the old man's generosity in deeding him CompuSoft, Joe wouldn't even be thinking about this for himself. Edmund had provided the means for Joe to spend the time needed to work on his program. With Edmund's death, that could have all ended for Joe, but it hadn't.

It was a dream come true.

Whether it was just his own bad luck or his unique ability to actually forget absolutely everything but his work, he entered his office and, completely unprepared, stared stupefied at the front desk.

It had been cleaned off, or rather cleared off—everything was on the floor. Amazing piles of important-looking stuff surrounded the base of the desk.

As he took a step into the chaotic room, he tripped and nearly fell flat on his face—over a pair of ruby-red four-inch pumps.

Empty pumps, he noted.

Which would explain the barefoot woman on all fours, facing away from him, affording him the best view he'd seen all morning. Apparently, both Tim and Andy felt the same way, because the two techs, who normally couldn't be budged from their computers, were on the floor, as well, making neat little stacks of God only knew what.

Caitlin's head popped up when he shut the door behind him, and she craned her neck around from where she'd been pulling out more stacks of paperwork from beneath her desk.

Hard as it was to imagine, Joe had completely forgotten about his new secretary.

"Good morning," she said in a sexy, cheerful voice that reminded him he still needed a cup of coffee.

Badly.

Tim and Andy leaped to their feet, faces red.

"Hey, Joe," Andy said quickly, sticking his hands in his jean pockets. "How'd it go at the bank?"

"It wasn't as exciting as it appears to have been here." Joe lifted a brow as Caitlin stretched her lush, petite body as far as it would reach to get a file that had been shoved beneath the far corner of her desk.

Tim's and Andy's jaws dropped open at the sight, but Joe could hardly blame them. He couldn't remember ever seeing a finer looking rear end.

And he'd seen his fair share.

But his quick surge of lust, coming on the heels of forgetting about his new secretary—whom he hadn't wanted in the first place—only further annoyed him. Already half the morning was gone, and by the looks of things nothing had been accomplished except for a shifting of the mess from the front desk to the floor.

He sighed.

Hadn't he known this would happen if he kept her?

And dammit, hadn't he asked her to wear something to hide that body?

Women, like his work, received his full attention. But they were also simply a diversion—a pleasant one, but temporary nonetheless.

It had to be that way.

He'd grown up in emotional chaos. *Painful* emotional chaos. That's what personal attachments did. Chopped up the heart and spit it back out. Brought nothing but the opportunity for hurt. With hurt came weakness, and he couldn't allow that.

He relied on himself, and that was it. He'd been remarkably relationship free. By choice. And any entanglements he'd enjoyed had been short but sweet.

An involvement with a co-worker couldn't be temporary, couldn't be short and sweet and therefore couldn't be contemplated. No matter how fine the…assets.

To prove it, he purposely turned his gaze away from the incredible sight before him.

Tim and Andy still stood there stupidly, gawking like teenagers. Joe opened his mouth to bark at them, but Vince appeared in the doorway, glasses on his nose, disk in hand.

"Guys," Vince said sternly. "You came out

here to check on Caitlin half an hour ago. What's going on—" He broke off at the sight that had rendered both Tim and Andy and then Joe speechless. Carefully, he closed his mouth. Then he glanced at Joe, both amusement and irritation swimming in his gaze.

Joe jerked his head sharply, and Vince nodded. "Tim, Andy, let's hit it."

Joe sighed when they disappeared and wondered exactly how long it would be before the socialite decided she didn't want to play at working anymore.

Hopefully very soon.

"Well, I beat you in," Caitlin announced, obviously expecting a medal.

"You should," he said, watching her wiggle up to her knees in the tightest, shortest, reddest skirt he'd ever seen. How had she gotten into that thing? "It's ten o'clock. What the hell are you doing?"

"Filing." She slapped her hands together to rid them of dust. "This place is a disaster. Don't you ever clean?"

"No, and I knew where everything is...*was*," he protested, trying not to panic.

"It'll be better," she promised him. "You'll see."

He doubted that and was about to tell her so but his phone rang. He watched, fascinated, as Caitlin stood and yanked down the short little jacket that matched her siren-red skirt before scooping up the receiver. "Hello?" Quickly, she covered the mouthpiece and batted her warm brown eyes at Joe. "Should I tell them this is CompuSoft?" she asked in a loud whisper. "Or is that redundant, do you think, since they called us and they most likely know who it is they dialed?" She bit her full, red bottom lip in indecision.

"Just find out who it is," Joe suggested through his teeth. "That might be a good place to start."

She nodded quite seriously and turned back to the phone. "Yes, who is this, please?" Her brow creased in concentration. Her hair settled around her flushed face. Then she lit up with the most dazzling smile Joe had ever seen. "Oh, isn't that sweet of you," she gushed. "I'm sure he'd love that, yes. Thanks so much." She hung up the phone and dropped back to her knees amid the mess she'd created all over his floor.

Joe found himself once again staring at her very cute wriggling butt. "Caitlin." His voice came out slightly strangled, and he had no idea if it were irritation or something more basic, such as his own software became hardware.

She stopped wriggling and smiled at him. "Yes, Mr. Brownley?"

He knew for a damn fact she was only eight years younger than him and she was calling him mister. "Joe."

"Okay. *Joe.*" She turned back to whatever the hell it was she thought she was doing.

"Who was on the phone?" he demanded.

"Oh. AT&T." She sent him that same dazzling smile, the one that did funny things to his knees. "They're going to send you a one-hundred-dollar credit for switching to their service for a trial period of two weeks. Isn't that sweet of them? Though you probably shouldn't have left them in the first place. I understand from that nice operator I just spoke with they have the best prices in the country."

Joe closed his eyes briefly and reminded himself that though he relied only on himself, rarely allowing another into his life, he *had* loved Edmund. He owed the man, and this woman—this crazy, out-of-control, messy woman—was his debt. "I'll be in my office," he managed to say finally.

She sent him a vague smile from where she was shuffling papers—*his* papers—around. "No problem."

As he turned to go, he tripped over her pumps, again.

SHE COULD DO THIS, Caitlin told herself. No problem. She'd gone through most of her life figuring things out by herself. She'd dealt with the death of her mother all those years ago. She'd dealt with traveling alone, celebrating holidays alone, generally being completely alone.

She could certainly answer a few phones and straighten up an office, especially since she didn't have much choice.

The bills had to be paid. She'd come home the

night before to several messages from credit collectors.

They were getting nasty.

The phones had been blissfully quiet for a while. So had the men, though they were checking on her often, which brought a smile. They were so sweet.

Except for Joe. No one in their right mind would call that powerfully built thug, masquerading as a mild-mannered computer geek, sweet.

She headed down the hallway to the small lunchroom, which held a refrigerator, a microwave, a sink and counter and a small table with chairs.

She glanced at the coffee machine and grimaced. Empty, of course. It would never occur to whoever had taken the last cup to make more. Automatically, her hostess skills leaping to life, she made the coffee. Then, because the room was disgusting, she cleaned it. Maybe, she thought as she scrubbed, she'd been looking at this all wrong. She was an organizer, and these men certainly needed her.

Needed her.

The mere idea stopped her cold. And warmed her heart. No one had ever needed her before.

"How's it going?"

Caitlin, her eyes still misty, smiled at Vince as he came in. "Good." She finished with the sponge on the counter and started sweeping.

"Really?" He didn't look convinced; he

looked worried. "I should congratulate you. You made it past the dreaded two-hour mark without quitting."

She thought of her late car payments. Of her rent, which was late, as well. She tried not to think of the stack of bills she'd filed away under her kitchen sink so she wouldn't have to look at them. "Oh, I'm not going to quit," she said with certainty.

"Well, that's a relief. You're like a ray of sunshine around here."

Caitlin glanced quickly at him, trying to decide if that had been a come-on. She'd become a pro at spotting them since she'd gotten curves at the tender age of twelve. But Vince simply smiled kindly. With that shock of deep red hair and Clark Kent–type glasses slipping down his nose, he was really kind of cute.

But Caitlin had decided long ago, the cute ones were *rarely* harmless. "That's me, just a ray of sunshine. I'm so bright you need sunglasses to look at me."

Vince laughed, but didn't make a move to come closer. Unbearably relieved to find someone *genuinely* nice, Caitlin relaxed. "Is it always so...uptight around here?" She graduated back to the sponge and wiped down the table that had an inch of grime on it.

"You mean Joe." Vince shook his head and leaned back against the sink, watching her clean with fascination. "He's just preoccupied. Ignore him. It's the best way." He frowned. "He didn't hurt your feelings, I hope, because he would hate that. He just doesn't have a wide focus. Work is pretty much all he concentrates on, and he really hates it when things get in the way of that."

"Well, someone should mention that work isn't everything in life."

"You handled him well."

"If that was well done, I'd hate to see him when he *isn't* handled properly."

"He's a good guy, Caitlin. Really. He's just under pressure right now. And he just lost Edmund—" He stopped, horrified. Color flooded his face. "I'm sorry. He was your father, so you know exactly how much Joe is hurting."

Yes, she knew and the thought of Joe mourning her father disconcerted and warmed her at the same time.

Joseph's grieving brought an image she hadn't anticipated and didn't know if she was ready to accept. "Which would explain how chipper he's been."

Vince let out a smile. "Well…truth is, he's just about always that way."

"But the rest of you—you and Tim and Andy—you're all so nice and welcoming. How do you do it?"

"Tim and Andy are really great. We've all been friends since…well, forever."

How wonderful those sort of ties must be. There was no one in her past with whom she kept in contact. "Tell me about all of you."

Vince laughed without embarrassment. "We were the proverbial school geeks. You know, the ones girls wouldn't even look at? Luckily, we'll get the last laugh. At our five-year reunion, we realized most of our school buddies are struggling with jobs like bagging groceries. Nothing beats this. Plus we still have hair."

She laughed. "And you're fit. At my reunion, the cheerleaders had gotten fat."

"See?" He grinned. "We're not fat. And we're doing what we love."

They were, Caitlin realized with a spurt of envy. She'd never found her place. She'd never really been satisfied. Maybe that was because she'd never really challenged herself, never held a real job.

That could change, she thought with hope. She could find her place. Maybe even right here.

The phone rang. "Just a sec," she said quickly, and then raced down the hall. "Good morning, CompuSoft— No, wait," she managed to say, breathless from her dash down the hall. "It's almost afternoon, now isn't it?" *Rambling.* A very unattractive trait. "Oh, forget it. Just hello."

She got a dial tone. "Well, hell."

"Nice phone manners."

Caitlin nearly leaped out of her skin at Joe's low, husky voice coming from directly behind her. Careful to roll her eyes *before* she turned to face him, she planted a smile on her lips. "So. You've come out of your cage."

"I smelled coffee—" He broke off abruptly when she suddenly shrugged out of her jacket.

Beneath the splashy red, she wore a sleeveless white silk blouse, pretty enough, and unremarkable but for the body beneath it. The soft material clung to her ripe curves in a way that made his pulse race. "What are you doing?" he demanded, backing up a step.

She laughed at the expression on his face. "Whatever you're thinking, that's not it." She dropped the jacket carelessly into her chair, kicked off her pumps and put her hands on her hips. "For your information, I just cleaned your filthy kitchen and I'm hot. Hence the jacket removal." She sent him a nasty look. "You guys are pigs."

She swung her hand out for emphasis and hit the lamp on the credenza.

Joe grabbed for it—a split second after it crashed to the floor, where it shattered into millions of jagged shards.

"Dammit!" he roared, falling to his knees besides his brand-new, very expensive zip drive. "What's this doing on the floor?"

"I was dusting. Do you have any idea how bad dust is for your computer?"

Strangling her was definitely wrong, he told himself. Carefully, he brushed away some of the lamp glass, but stabbed his thumb on a sharp, jagged piece. Swearing again, he pulled the sliver out of his skin and glared up at the woman who'd single-handedly brought chaos into his life.

Big mistake, looking up.

Kneeling at her feet, he found his face came to a very interesting level on her body. Interesting and erotic as hell. He forced his gaze past her tempting thighs, past the juncture between them, past the rest of her lovely curves and on to her unsettled, melting brown eyes.

"I'm sorry," she whispered, wringing her hands. "It's just that I'm—" Her stomach, inches from his face, growled noisily. "Hungry," she finished lamely. "I'm...very hungry."

Joe closed his eyes. "You're hungry."

"Yes." She nodded emphatically, pressing her hands to her belly.

At that moment, Vince walked in, his gaze widening slightly at Joseph's and Caitlin's suggestive pose. "Did I interrupt something?"

"Just me about to get fired," Caitlin said with a sigh.

Tim and Andy pushed their curious way into the front office, too.

"What's wrong?" Andy asked, after taking note of Joseph's fierce scowl.

"Everything," Joe said, glaring at Caitlin.

"It's really been nice knowing you guys," said Caitlin, smiling shakily at the three techs.

"Wait," Vince said quietly. He looked at Joe. "Wait a minute. Don't do anything rash."

"Yeah, Joe," Tim piped up. "You can't fire her. She made coffee. *Great* coffee."

"And she cleaned," Andy added. "Did you know the tile in the kitchen is *white?*"

Instead of detonating, as Caitlin fully expected, Joe just shook his head.

Then burst out laughing. A full, rich, very pleasant and contagious sound she'd never expected of him. While everyone stared at him, he laughed so hard, he doubled over, hands on his thighs.

Caitlin didn't get the joke. "I'm sorry about the zip drive," she whispered.

Silence. Apparently, for once not even Tim, Andy or Vince had anything positive or hopeful to say.

Instead, they all looked in unison at Joe, their expressions filled with the uneasy worry one gives another before shipping him off to the mental ward.

Joe sniffed, straightened, took a deep breath and said, "Well, shit. I guess it's lunchtime."

"Really, Joe?"

He looked directly at Caitlin, his eyes hooded. "Yeah. What the hell."

Relief and hope surged, made her laugh a little giddily. In that moment, Caitlin forgot that he didn't like silly, untrained women, and that she didn't like hard, know-it-all men who looked too tasty for their own good.

Maybe, just maybe, this would work out after all.

That's when the coffeemaker, still plugged in, burst into flames.

4

LUNCH SHOULD HAVE been simple. After they'd gotten rid of the fire department, the five of them—Vince, Tim, Andy, Joe and Caitlin—all piled into Vince's van.

But Tim and Andy couldn't decide on a place, and Vince kept making the wrong turn when Joe would call out directions. This would have normally greatly amused Caitlin, except for the fact she was pressed up close in the seat next to Joe.

Actually, plastered was more like it.

She found it a bit unsettling to feel the solid power of him against her, to realize how big he really was. And given the rigid way he held himself so as to minimize contact, he was obviously every bit as aware of her as she was of him.

"Wait! *That* way," Tim yelled, and the van swerved as Vince made the turn.

Caitlin could feel the strain in Joseph's body as he tried to remain completely upright and away from her. He didn't quite succeed and at the next quick turn, which came without warning, he had to lift an arm to the back of her seat to brace himself rather than fall directly on her. Still, his jean-clad thigh pressed against her.

Their sides were glued together. She was surrounded by him, by his warmth, by his strength.

He smelled like burned coffee.

"Sorry," he said gruffly, and tried to pull back just as the van turned in the opposite direction, landing Caitlin practically in his lap.

"It's okay." She shot him a smile in spite of how her stomach tightened as the bare skin of his sinewy, tanned arm rubbed against her softer, much lighter one.

Their gazes met and Caitlin's smile faded. So did Joseph's. She pulled back, straightened herself. Joe withdrew his arm from around her, but he moved slowly, and she felt his fingers trace lightly over the back of her neck as he did.

She shivered.

Joe frowned at his hand as if he'd lost control of it and if he felt half of what she had begun to feel, then she completely understood.

THEY ENDED UP at one of her favorite restaurants.

Only problem was, everyone in southern California apparently wanted to eat there, too. Her nerves immediately reacted to the thought of waiting for a table in the packed bar, pressed tight against the man she tried to convince herself she disliked.

Caitlin would never be sure how it happened, but somehow she ended up at a cozy table for two—with Joe. The others had gotten a table on the other side of the restaurant, quickly and eagerly abandoning her in their haste for pasta.

Joe, looking slightly pained—and who could blame him? Caitlin wondered wildly—tried valiantly to smile at her.

She couldn't dredge one up in return. "I'm sorry about the coffeemaker."

"The fire chief said it wasn't your fault," he reminded her. "The cord was frayed, just a fire waiting to happen."

"Yes," she said miserably, blocking out the pleasantly noisy crowd around them. "But the zip drive...can't blame that on a frayed cord."

"It's done, Caitlin. Forget it."

She froze, stared at him over her menu. "What?"

"I said, it's done. Forget it."

"No." She shook her head. "Not that. The other."

"What other?"

"You used my name," she breathed, some of her innate good humor returning. "Without that big old frown on your face."

"No, I didn't."

"You did so. Oops, never mind. The frown is back."

They sat in silence. After a moment, Joe asked, "Was there something wrong with me being friendly?"

"No. Not at all. It was kinda...nice. Unexpected, but nice."

"I don't mean to be...unnice."

"I know." And she did. Somehow, she just brought out the worst in him.

He started to lift his water glass, but looked at his hand with a small wince instead.

"Oh, Joe, you're hurt from the glass! I'd forgotten." Grabbing his hand, she studied the base of his thumb. A cut marred the tough skin.

"It's nothing." He tried to pull his hand back, but she held firm as guilt and regret washed over her.

"I know I keep saying this," she told him. "But I'm so sorry." Without thinking, she lifted his hand to her mouth and kissed his palm, directly beneath the injury. "There."

Joe blinked, stunned, as heat and something far more purled low in his gut. Those full red lips lingered on his skin, making him instantly hard. He had to remind himself that he was reacting naturally to the outer package that made up Caitlin. Not the inner one—the airhead, the destroyer of offices. He cleared his throat. "Is that supposed to make it better?"

That quirky, contagious grin of hers crossed her face. "I think so. Or at least, I hope so. I always..." Her smile faded. "I always wanted someone to do that to my hurts. Silly, huh?"

That quick, sharp pang in his chest was heartburn—*not* in any way empathy. He assured himself of this. Promised himself. "No, it's not silly."

"Did it work? Does it feel better?"

Hard to tell, since the ache had settled in his chest, thick and unmovable. Joseph's world had been lived alone. Always alone. He'd learned early he could rely on no one but himself. *No one.* Not the authorities, not his friends and certainly not his parents. Anything he'd needed or wanted, he'd gotten on his own.

Like Caitlin, he'd once dreamed about having someone kiss away his pains. No one, to his recollection, had ever given a damn about him, not until her father had come along and dragged him off the fast track to nowhere. Edmund had saved his sorry hide, had been the first one to care, and now his daughter was staring at him with those huge dark eyes, wanting him to feel better even though it'd been *she* who'd turned his world upside down. "Yeah," he told her. "It worked."

Her beaming smile dazzled him, only this time his reaction was far more than just physical. It went deeper, and he didn't think he liked it.

He didn't want to feel this strange softening toward her. She was everything he couldn't stand. Unmotivated. With a serious lack of ambition. Little common sense. With Edmund as her father, she'd had the world at her fingertips and what had she done? Thrown parties. Just remembering these things made him suitably irritated all over again, allowing him to forget that he'd almost, *almost*, started to like her.

Purposely, he hardened his face into the expression he knew could terrorize the toughest of souls. That should scare her. Keep him safe.

She smiled at him.

Dammit. How was he supposed to deal with that?

Around them, life continued to the music of clinking glasses and tinkling china. Voices sounded, some low and muted, some not. Laughter. And the smells… In another time and place, his surroundings might have fascinated him; he enjoyed watching people.

Today, he had eyes for only one person, and that bugged him. He stayed tucked behind his menu, pretending to scrutinize the list of entrées he had already memorized. What was happening to him?

It was her clothes—that's what. Her amazing eyes. That infectious laugh. They were all designed to attract a man. Clearly, she enjoyed being looked at.

Knowing this about her helped him control the lust, because if he ever decided he wanted more than a passing fancy with a woman, which he wouldn't, it would be with one who wanted *him*. It would be with a woman who didn't send out signals to anything in pants. A woman who loved him heart and soul—him and only him.

This woman could do none of those things, and telling himself so helped. A little. But nothing could control his lethal curiosity. "Tell me about your father."

She looked startled, then she shrugged. "You knew him better than me, so there's nothing to tell." She set her menu down and before he could continue his line of questioning, she said, "Joe, about your kitchen."

"Don't remind me," he groaned, picking up his glass of water.

"I'll clean it up."

"No," he said quickly, setting down the glass to lift his hands. "I'll do it."

"And your zip drive. I'm so sorry."

"I said forget it."

"Why didn't you fire me?"

He'd wanted to. It had been the first thought that popped into his mind at the time, but he couldn't very well tell her that. He knew he was difficult sometimes, but he never purposely hurt anyone.

"Joe?"

The menu again held his interest for a long moment before he slowly lowered it. "It's best if we drop this now."

"Why?"

The waitress came up to them, and because they both knew what they wanted, she took their menu shields, leaving Joe feeling strangely exposed. Vulnerable.

"Why, Joe?"

Spreading his big hands on the table, he stared at them. "I'll tell you on one condition. No, make that two. First, you don't take this personally, and second, after I tell you, you have to be honest back and tell me why someone with your wealth and means would want this job in the first place."

Humiliating as it would be to disclose her predicament, she had to know. "Deal."

His light blue eyes penetrated hers. "I *can't* fire you. I promised your father I'd give you a job. It's in the will."

The waitress brought their food, and Joe dug in.

Caitlin stared at him helplessly. "I don't understand. The will doesn't say 'for as long as I want it.' All it says is that you'll *hire* me."

"So much for not taking this personally." He sighed and set down his fork. "Yes, but I promised him."

"When?"

"Before he died. He'd been having health problems."

He'd never told her. She'd never asked. Guilt stabbed at her.

"It seemed to mean a lot to him that you have this job, so I went along with it."

She managed to speak evenly. "You don't strike me as a man who'd go along with anything that didn't suit your purposes, Joe."

"Since that's pretty much true, I suppose there's no use in being insulted." But his jaw was tight as he lifted his glass to his lips. "Let's just call it the repaying of a debt, and in this case, despite any trouble you might cause, I could hire you for the rest of your life and not make a dent in what I owe him."

The image of her father came to mind—powerful, busy, always gone. Much as he'd given her in material things, he'd rarely had time for anything else. It was hard to imagine him inspiring this kind of fierce loyalty. "What is this great thing he did for you?"

"He rescued me." When she just stared at him in surprise, he said, "Twenty years ago, he took a twelve-year-old know-it-all street kid out of an alley where he was about to be killed by a gang-banger for hustling him."

"Were you the twelve-year-old or the gang-banger?"

He grinned, his first, and it was a stunner. "The former."

But Caitlin didn't see the humor. She was horrified, picturing a poor, thin, starving kid fighting off a dangerous thug—no matter she'd thought of Joe as a thug himself earlier that day. "Where were your parents?"

He shrugged broad shoulders. "I never knew my father, and there were six kids. My mother couldn't feed us all. I'd been pretty much on my own for a couple of years."

"Oh, Joe. I'm sorry."

"I turned out all right," he said, lowering his head and shoveling in more food. He smiled suddenly, and the charm of it surprised her. She kept forgetting how good-looking he was, behind all that attitude. "Edmund cleaned me up and hauled me off to a Laker game."

Her jaw dropped. To her knowledge, her father had been too busy for sports. He'd certainly never taken *her* to a game. "He did?"

"Yeah." He smiled at the memory. "They won, too. Then he dumped me in a tough school designed for...troubled kids."

"And for really smart ones, too, I'll bet."

Joseph's head jerked up, his eyes hot and defensive. "Yeah," he said finally, as though it was a hard thing to admit.

Now it made sense, all too well. She knew how attractive a homeless, orphaned, incredibly brilliant *boy* would have been to her father. Especially when all he'd gotten was a weak, not so smart female. Resentment hit, only to be beaten back by shame.

What would have happened to Joe if her father hadn't intervened?

"He came for me every weekend, which at first really ticked me off," Joe admitted. "But he stuck with me until the end." He met her gaze unwaveringly. "He saved my life, princess. I owe him everything, and in return, I'd do anything for him."

Including putting up with a secretary he didn't want. Suddenly feeling a little sick and unbearably lonely even in the middle of a crowded restaurant, Caitlin set down her fork and tried to ignore the tightness in her chest. How pathetic her poor-little-rich-girl story would seem to him. "What happened to your mother?"

He chugged down his water and attacked the basket of bread sticks. "She lives in Vegas. Waitresses occasionally."

"And the others? Your brothers and sisters?"

His blue eyes became shuttered, and she imagined he masked pain and loneliness. "Scattered around." His gaze dropped to the bread he held, which he then polished off in one bite.

She learned far more about Joe by watching his eyes than listening to his words. His eyes were much more expressive than he could possibly know. "Do you ever see them?"

"They're all busy with their own lives. My mother calls me once in a while."

Caitlin swallowed hard, hurting for the boy who'd grown up too fast. Who'd learned to count only on himself. "You support her, don't you?"

He stirred, clearly uncomfortable. "Maybe."

"Why is it so hard to admit you help her?"

"Why is it so hard for you to understand that most people don't like their lives to be an open book?"

She was beginning to realize the man was all bark, no bite. He liked his distance. Too bad she didn't do the distance thing so well.

Joe fell silent as he continued to feed himself with obvious relish, making Caitlin wonder where he put all the food. He certainly didn't have a spare ounce of fat on him. She glanced up, and caught the curious gazes of Vince, Tim and Andy from across the room. The twins grinned at her. Vince's smile was more subdued, worried.

Sweet, she thought. *And chicken.* She stuck her tongue out at them, and they laughed.

Joe polished off his plate and glanced at hers. "Are you going to finish?"

If she drew a deep breath, she'd pop the button on her tight skirt. "No." He continued to gaze longingly at the lasagna left on her plate. Laughing, she pushed it toward him, then watched in amazement as he finished it off.

"To be honest," Joe told her when he'd finally filled himself. "I never thought you'd actually take the job."

Here it comes, she thought. His scorn. And after learning about him and his past, she knew she deserved every bit of it. She took a deep breath. "I need this job."

"Right."

"It's true. I'm deeply in debt, and without the income, meager as it is, I'll be homeless and on the streets just like you once were."

He stared at her. "No way."

"Yes way." She played with her water glass. "Those assets you spoke of that first day, my car and my place, they haven't been paid for. As you know, they're far out of my league with what you're paying me. I'm flat broke."

"What about the will?"

"What about it? I got nothing."

"Then why did Edmund stipulate such a low salary? He was the most generous man I know."

She shrugged, even managed a light smile, but Joe wasn't fooled. Pain blazed from her eyes.

"Maybe he just didn't realize?" he suggested.

"Whether he realized or not doesn't matter," she said. "The sorry truth is, this job is all I have, and I desperately need it. I know you hate it, Joe, and to tell you the truth, so do I. There's just not much choice in the matter at the moment."

Dammit. Dammit all to hell. He didn't want to feel this quick, inexplicable tug of concern, of protectiveness, shame because he'd gotten from Edmund what his own daughter hadn't. "He didn't mean to hurt you." He could bank on that.

"You think so?" She lifted those huge, liquid eyes to his. "Even when I'm a spoiled *princess*? Always had the world at my fingertips? Isn't that what you've thought all along?" She smiled humorlessly at his wince. "But you know what? All I really wanted was his time. How's that for spoiled? He had you, though, and that was all he needed."

Lunch lodged in his throat. "I gather you weren't close."

"Don't pretend that you two didn't talk about me. I know what he thought of my life-style."

How to tell her that Edmund had rarely spoken of her at all, and only at the very end? Clearly, he didn't have to tell her; she'd looked at his face and seen the truth.

"I must seem double pathetic now."

"No," he said, leaning close, disturbed by that protectiveness he felt. "Caitlin..."

"Don't apologize for him. It was my fault, too.

I didn't see him much because of our respective business schedules. And don't," she said quickly, raising a hand. "Don't make some crack about poor little socialite me. If you're thinking I had it pretty good, you're right. I did. I never had to live on the streets, fighting for my life, and I certainly never went hungry or without clothes. But I also never had what I really wanted, which was someone to tell me they loved me."

Joe hadn't thought, hadn't wondered…all those times he and Edmund spent together, he had never thought to ask about Edmund's daughter, or where she was. "I'm sorry," he murmured, well aware of the inadequacy of those words.

"Don't be sorry for me." She tucked a loose wave of hair behind her ear and gave him a look from beneath lowered lashes that he couldn't quite read. "I'm just glad I still have a job."

He looked at the woman who had cheerfully and without complaint thrown herself wholeheartedly into a job that had been forced on her. She'd genuinely tried hard, even when out of her element. She'd given it her all.

Damn. He pulled his thoughts up short. He'd done it again. Just one bright, open smile and he'd folded. One bat of those long lashes and he was willing to forget that he could hardly tolerate her. Purposefully, he hardened himself. "All I need you to do is answer the phones, Caitlin. *Nothing else. Just* the phones," he said, leaning forward to make his point, grabbing her hand when she ignored him. He thought of how his office looked once she'd started to organize it. "Promise me."

Her voice filled with wounded pride, she countered, "I can do more, far more, if you'd teach me."

The waitress saved him from replying, and he was grateful. She tactfully set down their bill almost in the center of the table, but slightly closer to Joe.

He picked up the slip, reaching for his wallet and scanning the balance at the same time. "Eighteen-fifty," he muttered to himself. "With a tip that's—"

"Two dollars and seventy-eight cents," Caitlin whispered politely, leaning forward discreetly. "But leave three-seventy instead."

"What?"

"Twenty percent." Caitlin was leaning close enough to daze him with that light, sexy scent she wore. "You should leave twenty percent since we got such great service." She opened her purse and he put a hand over hers, halting her.

"Wait a minute." He shook his head to clear it, then gazed back into guileless eyes the color of milk chocolate. "Are you telling me you can multiply in your head like that, instantly?"

Caitlin flashed him a self-conscious smile. "Uh...yes. I'm sorta good with numbers. Big ones." She shrugged. "It's a semiuseless talent."

"Are you kidding?"

"Well, it does come in handy when I'm shopping in Mexico City and trying to figure out the exchange rate."

Again he shook his head, counting out bills.

"Twenty-two dollars and twenty cents," she said helpfully.

"Amazing," he said, dropping the cash in the tray and handing it up to the waiting server.

Caitlin was staring solemnly at him.

"What now? You thinking about calculating the national debt?"

She shook her head. "I've never had to support myself before, Joseph. And I realize I'm spoiled. But that's going to change." She let out a little laugh. "It has to, actually. I don't have any money."

"Maybe a loan," he said desperately. "They have them everywhere now. All the banks..."

"I want to work."

"There are other jobs, other things you could do that would suit you better."

"I'm not a quitter, Joe." Determination and pure grit shimmered off her, and her voice was soft yet strong and even, completely without rancor. "I just need a little time to prove myself. And if you don't have the inclination to give me the time I need, then I'm sure Andy and Tim and Vince will."

She had *that* right, he thought as he glanced at the three cohorts, all staring across the room directly at Caitlin, stars sparkling in their eyes.

Caitlin scooted back from the table and rose

with wounded dignity. Every male eye in the place was instantly on her. Every eye but Joe's.

He was lost in thoughts of her determination and grit—two of his favorite qualities. He almost liked her, he realized with some surprise.

How many people could he say that about?

5

CAITLIN GOT UP the next morning and discovered two unpleasant things. One, if she wanted to eat again in the near future, she was going to have to ask Joe how often she got paid. Weekly, she hoped as she stared with dismay into her nearly empty refrigerator thinking that, given a sorry choice of expired cottage cheese or a mustard sandwich on stale bread, payday couldn't be soon enough.

Two, and even more important, her car was gone. Missing. Vanished from the face of the earth.

Just the thought had her hyperventilating. Her BMW, her pride and joy, the one thing her father had given her that she knew he'd bought with her in mind... Well, he hadn't actually paid for it outright, but up until his death, he'd given her the money for the lease and insurance.

She'd already called the police when it occurred to her that she might have missed a few payments.

It wasn't her fault, really. She'd been so busy. First in Paris with a girlfriend for holiday shopping. Then in Mexico at another friend's resort for Christmas. She'd come home in time for New Year's Eve at the Comedy Club.

Then her father had died, and both her so-called friends *and* her money had disappeared.

Well, at least she hadn't been kicked out of her condo yet. That was something, wasn't it?

CAITLIN HAD NEVER in her life had to rely on public transportation. It was every bit the adventure she'd thought it would be and more. And so, of course, she was late.

She dashed through the foyer, waved to Amy, leaped on the elevator and stumbled into the office at ten o'clock to face a not-so-happy-looking Joe Brownley.

"How nice of you to grace us with your presence," he said overly politely.

Usually, nothing flattened her faster than disapproval, but she wasn't in the mood. Not today. She thought about telling him so, but stopped when she realized that, given how he'd grown up, he might not be exactly sympathetic to her losing the BMW she hadn't paid for in the first place.

"I'm sorry I'm a little late—"

"A little?" He let out a short laugh and shook his head. "Princess, there are going to have to be rules in this…this…"

"Relationship?" she suggested sweetly, making him scowl even deeper.

"*Office.* This is *not* a relationship," he said stiffly. "It's a job. You come in at eight like the rest of us. In the *morning,*" he added with emphasis.

He wore black jeans today. And a black polo shirt, untucked as usual. It stretched tight across his broad shoulders and snugged his hard, lean chest. With his hands on his hips and that scowl on his handsome face, he looked like a modern-day pirate, capable of pillaging along with the best of them.

She definitely should not have stayed up late reading that fantastic lusty historical romance. The pirate hero had tossed the heroine over his shoulder and stalked with her into his private cabin, where he'd tossed the passionate but virginal redhead on his berth and—

"*What* is that?" her pirate demanded, pointing to her outfit.

Caitlin glanced down at herself, but saw nothing wrong with her canary-yellow captain's jacket and matching short full skirt, or her equally yellow high-heeled pumps. She'd needed the extra height this morning to boost her lagging confidence and stomped-on spirits.

She would have preferred an expensive shopping trip to Italy, but beggars couldn't be choosers.

Of course, no one had told her she'd have to walk nearly a mile—*twice*—to catch connecting buses.

Tomorrow, she was wearing her crosstrainers.

She'd only gotten on the wrong bus once. Okay, twice, but that second time hadn't been her fault.

"What's wrong with my clothes?" she asked.

"Everything!"

She looked again, just to make sure she'd buttoned all her buttons and didn't have toilet paper stuck to her shoe, but everything was just fine. "What?"

His sigh exploded out of him as he turned away. "Nothing."

"It's something."

He whipped around to face her, plowing his fingers through his hair. His raised arms, stretched, tightened, and made her mouth go dry because he was so...

"You said you'd wear...*more,*" he said at last.

She laughed. "No, I never said that. *You* did."

He closed his eyes, a habit she'd noticed he fell back on when frustrated or furious, both seemingly constant elements of his charming personality. "I asked nicely," he said, his voice strained.

"You most definitely did not."

"Please," he said after a moment. "Please, wear more. *Lots* more."

"Is that a rule, too?"

His eyes flashed and she didn't miss the quick humor they revealed. "If I said yes, would you follow it?"

She grinned back. "Probably not. I don't do the authority thing too well."

His gaze became serious. "This isn't going to work."

"It will if you stop bellowing."

He went still. "I haven't yelled at you."

"You raised your voice when I dropped the lamp on your thingie."

"Zip drive," he said through his teeth. "It was a *zip drive*, princess. A very expensive one. And I didn't yell—I nearly cried!"

"You're doing it again."

His shoulders slumped. "I'm sorry. I tend to talk loud when I get— Never mind. Christ! How the hell do you always get me so off track?"

"You were picking on me."

"I was not picking on you." He stopped, drew a deep, ragged breath. "Forget the zip drive, okay? Just answer the phone. Nothing else."

She thought of his disastrous files, which she had started to organize. She could have the office fully operational in no time. "But—"

"No *buts*."

He hadn't fired her.

This man was not nearly as tough as he thought he was, which made her smile. She would fix his office, and he'd see just how valuable she could be.

He'd need her then…and she liked the sound of that.

"Now—" he pointed to the phone "—there are two lines, and the first one—"

"Thank you, Joe," she interrupted softly, laying her hand over his.

He yanked his hand back and scowled. "Pay attention. Our phones are ringing off the hook right now because of the merger. A lot of our customers—"

"Customers?"

"We design and sell software. We also provide the tech support."

"That's what Tim, Andy and Vince do?"

He nodded. "Among other things. Just find out who it is they need to speak to. Put them on Hold, then use the intercom in our offices and we'll pick up." He pointed to another series of buttons, but Caitlin's mind began to wander. She lifted her head and encountered the most expressive light blue eyes she'd ever seen. "Do you wear contacts?" she wondered out loud.

"Caitlin." His nostrils flared. "You're not paying attention."

Paying attention was hard when he was so darn magnificent. He stood there, leaning over her, wearing that fierce expression—his jaw all tight and his sexy mouth hard—and suddenly, she wanted to kiss him.

Bad idea, she decided, and ducked her head. "I'm sorry. I'm listening now."

Vince came out of his office, took one look at Joseph's tense face and changed directions from the kitchen to Caitlin's desk. "Joe," he said quietly, "Tim needs you. He's having trouble with a control panel and wanted me to let you know."

"He'll have to wait a minute." Joe rubbed his temples. "I'm training Caitlin."

Caitlin's stomach tightened uncomfortably with the now familiar feeling of stress. She hated it.

"I'll help her," Vince suggested, tactfully slipping in between Joe and Caitlin and giving her a shy smile. "After all, I'm the one who trained the last hundred secretaries you scared off. What's one more?"

There was her hero, Caitlin thought. Too bad his smile didn't stop her heart like Joseph's did.

"Good luck," muttered the modern-day pirate as he escaped scot-free.

"Don't worry about him." Vince grinned, which went a long way to relieve Caitlin's tension. "He doesn't have much patience. He's far too focused."

"Well, I hope he focuses somewhere else this morning while I organize this place. It's a disaster."

"Um…maybe you shouldn't."

He was worried and it made her smile. "I can do this. You'll see."

"But Joe—"

"Doesn't know how good I am." She patted his hand. "You'll see," she repeated.

TIM AND ANDY CAME through a short time later, looking for fun, as they always did on their break.

Tim toed the controlled mess she had on the office floor, and whistled slowly. "What'd Joe say about this?"

Caitlin had to smile. "After complaining about how late I was, and then my clothes, he sort of ran out of steam. I'm sure he'll get to it the next time he happens by, but I'm hoping to file all this away by then."

Tim looked nervous. "Maybe I should help you," he suggested. "No use riling him up."

He was afraid she'd get herself fired, and it was so sweet she smiled in spite of her own nerves. Besides, she refused to put Joe in a position where his men had divided loyalties. She'd caused enough trouble. "I've got it covered," she assured him.

"What's wrong with your clothes?" Andy wanted to know, looking her over in frank appreciation. "They look plenty good to me."

"He said I needed *more*," Caitlin told him. Both Tim and Andy protested loudly, only to fall completely silent when Joe came into the front office.

He took one look at them hanging around the reception desk, and his jaw went impossibly tight.

Caitlin imagined he'd have quite a headache if he kept it up. "I've got the phone down pat, boss," she said sweetly.

"Terrific." Joe glanced pointedly at the two techs, and they scattered, each offering muttered excuses.

Caitlin's stomach growled, loudly, into the silent office.

Joe raised an eyebrow. "Hungry again?"

"My stomach's funny that way. You'd think since I ate so much yesterday, it'd still be satisfied."

He frowned. "You haven't eaten since yesterday?"

That wasn't quite what she'd meant to say, but now that she thought about it, she'd only snacked last night on the last of a stale bag of pretzels. She'd never gotten to dinner.

Then, this morning, she'd skipped breakfast because of her missing car, not to mention an empty fridge. What with bus hopping, she'd been too upset to eat anything, not that she'd had much choice by then.

Joe sighed at her silence, took her arm and pulled her up out of her chair. They headed for the door. "Come on," he said gruffly.

"Where?"

"To feed you, dammit." They were in the hallway, walking at his pace, which was nearly a run for Caitlin in her heels, when her stomach growled again.

Joseph's own stomach tightened as he remembered all too well what hunger felt like. "How did you make it this far without a keeper?" he demanded abruptly.

Under his hand, her arm went rigid. So did the rest of her. "I had one, but he died." She yanked her arm free and met his steady gaze. "Remember?"

Yeah, he remembered. And now she was looking for another keeper. He refused to be it. Horrified that he'd nearly fallen into that position because he'd felt sorry for her, he backed up a step. *Distance.* He desperately needed distance.

"Don't worry, Joe." Her smile was brittle. "Even if I wanted another 'keeper,' you'd be the last man on earth I'd choose."

Heels clicking, hips swaying, attitude popping, she moved away from him, down the hallway.

Out of some sick need to continue sparring with her, he followed her.

The elevator ride was silent and awkward, with her throwing mental daggers and him deflecting them. When the doors opened, she left without a word.

Again he followed.

Outside the office building, she took a deep breath, then jumped a little when she saw him. "Do you miss him?" she asked suddenly.

He didn't have to ask who, and yes, God, how he missed him.

The streets were filled with lunch-hour traffic, both motorists and pedestrians. The crowd was busy, noisy...and impolite. People shoved past them, around them, mumbling and grumbling as they went on with their day.

"Do you?" she asked quietly.

"Yes." He swallowed past the familiar stab of pain. "I miss him a lot."

She nodded and watched the people. The light breeze tossed her short skirt about her incredible thighs. Joseph's unhappy thoughts shifted and he concentrated on her body. When she crossed her arms tightly over her middle, her full breasts strained against the material of her jacket, making serious thought difficult, if not impossible.

"I do, too," she admitted so quietly he was forced to lean closer. Now her exotic, sexy scent teased him, and he inhaled deeply, torturing himself.

"But I don't understand…why did he do this to me?"

Edmund had served her a direct hit, and Joe felt uncomfortable with her grief and confusion, because he was just as grief stricken and confused.

"You were friends with him," she said. "You were friends, but we aren't."

She was fishing. She needed, yearned…and he ached for her, but he'd never told a lie in his life, not even to save someone's feelings, and he wouldn't start now. "I'm sorry."

She looked at him, accepting his silent admission that no, they were not friends. "I want us to get along."

How to tell her that he didn't? That he "got along" with very few people, and he liked it that way. That the only reason he ever "got along" with a beautiful woman was to "get it on."

"I don't want to be someone you have to baby-sit."

"That's good. Because I don't baby-sit," he said.

"You were dragging me off to feed me," she pointed out, ignoring a nasty remark from a harassed-looking woman who had to walk around them on the sidewalk. "I work for you from eight to five, but what I do before or after shouldn't be your concern."

"Then eat, dammit!"

"Yeah, that sort of...um...reminds me..." She bit her lip. "How often do we get paid?"

All his annoyance fled as he stared at her. His stomach suddenly hurt. "Are you *that* out of money?"

She paused. Shrugged. "Sort of, yeah."

Damn. "Today. You'll get paid today."

"I don't want your pity. I just want to know when we get paid around here. Weekly, bi-weekly, what?"

"Don't," he said harshly, and when she flinched he lightened his tone with effort. "I know what it's like to be hungry, to not eat because there's no food." He rubbed his belly, almost feeling that bone-gnawing hunger from his youth all over again. God, he hated this. A little panicked now, because she made him feel things he didn't want to, he shoved his hand into his pocket and pulled out whatever bills he had in there, slapping them into her palm. "Take this. It's an advance."

Horrified, she glanced downward, then pushed the money back at him. "No. I'm not the local charity case."

"Take it." He shoved the money into her jacket pocket. A mistake. Through the material, he could feel her warm flesh.

"I told you yesterday that I can do this," she

said a little shakily as she backed away from him. "I can handle being on my own just fine. I don't think you believe that, but it's true, and I'm going to prove it to you." As she took another step back, she enunciated each word. "*I can take care of myself.*"

"Wait," he called out when she turned and took off down the street.

Of course she didn't wait. She never did as he asked.

He could have caught her easily. In those ridiculously high heels, she was hardly moving faster than a quick stroll, but he knew she needed to be alone. She'd resent him intruding now. It would hurt her pride. And he knew all about pride.

Still… He hadn't meant to hurt her feelings, but he just kept doing it. He hated how that made him feel.

Why, Edmund? he wondered for the umpteenth time. *Why have you done this to me?*

Vince came up beside him, watching Caitlin disappear into the crowd. "You have such a touch with women, Joe," he said dryly.

"Hey, most of them like me."

"None of them 'like' you. They *want* you. Some for money, some for that reputed charm of yours, but none of them because they *like* you."

Someone else might have taken offense to Vince's honesty, but Joe always appreciated it. "Look who's talking," he countered. "I don't see you married or anything."

"But you will." Vince stared into the crowd where Caitlin had disappeared. "You will." A muscle twitched in his cheek. "Tell me you didn't fire her."

"We've done fine without a secretary before."

Joe and Vince went way back, but Joe had, in all that time, never seen Vince's temper. He saw it now. The redhead flushed from roots to neck, and his eyes narrowed. "I can't believe you did it," he said furiously. "Fired another one! And she was the nicest, sweetest one we ever had."

"Sweet?" Joe laughed. "Nothing that looks that good is sweet, believe me."

Vince was disgusted. "If I didn't know better, Joe, I'd say she scares you."

"She terrifies me. She's going to destroy our office."

"You know what I mean."

"I didn't fire her, Vince," he said wearily.

Vince relaxed marginally. "But you wanted to."

"Look, I'm stuck with her because of a stupid promise. Yeah, I wanted to."

"No, that's not it—it's not the promise," Vince said as he studied his longtime friend. "I know you better than that. You're running scared." He shook his head in amazement. "And I thought you were fearless."

"I'm not afraid of her."

"Uh-huh. Well, whatever you do, don't hurt her. I like her."

Vince's voice gave away nothing, but the way

his eyes were trained on Caitlin's disappearing figure in the crowd did. Not that Joe cared, but Vince clearly *did* like Caitlin. A lot.

He'd probably even ask her out eventually, Joe thought, his gut tightening yet again.

Caitlin would probably say yes.

Dammit. He really hated working with women.

6

FOR ONE ENTIRE AFTERNOON, Caitlin didn't see Joe. He was at meetings with the bank, with customers, with who knew whom else.

She was thankful for the respite, which gave her the peace and quiet and nerve to do as she'd threatened. She'd reorganized all the files and now everything was clean, tidy and in its place.

By chance, she'd intercepted the bank statement for the business checking account when it had arrived in the mail. Because numbers had always mysteriously called her, she went ahead and reconciled his statement on her break. She would have and could have easily closed out the month, but picturing Joseph's face, she didn't quite dare.

Vince, Tim and Andy were thrilled with the way the office looked, and how smoothly everything was running. It was amazing how big the place seemed once the floors were clear and it wasn't like walking through a maze just to cross the rooms. Caitlin had no idea how Joe would feel about it, but she could bet he wouldn't offer the joy and easy acceptance she'd gotten from the techs.

However he reacted, he couldn't avoid her

forever, or discount that strange, unaccountable attraction between them that flared up at the most annoying of times.

Every time they looked at each other, there were sparks.

It went deeper than the physical, far deeper, for there existed between them a bond she couldn't deny, and it made her as wary of him as he was of her.

Caitlin was studiously avoiding any serious relationships out of self-preservation. She knew from experience with her father and her fair-weather friends that close relationships brought only pain. Disappointment. Loneliness.

Being on her own was better. Easier.

Either Joe had learned that lesson, too, or he simply didn't like her.

That day he'd given her an advance from his own pocket, she'd come back from her lunch break to find a paycheck on her desk, handwritten by him. The gesture hadn't surprised her. Beneath his rough and tough exterior, she had a feeling he was a big softie.

She laughed at herself. A softie. *Right.*

Well, now she had one paycheck and her pride. It was the latter that allowed her to keep a stiff upper lip in those dark moments when despair threatened, when she cried herself to sleep thinking about her father and the way he'd abandoned her.

She knew all her father's assets were gone, divided among his friends and associates, but she didn't know why. For the first time, she decided she deserved answers. She called his attorney, but because he was out of town for the next week, she had to leave a message.

Feeling marginally better, Caitlin sat on her bed and reviewed her mail. It was a particularly bad mail day, each envelope hiding a big, ugly, nasty bill, all of which were at least second notices.

But the last one really caught her eye—a notice to vacate her condo.

The bank was finally going to sell.

She'd known this moment would come sooner or later, but she'd been hoping for later, *much* later.

Why, she wondered for the thousandth time, hadn't her father paid off her car or her condo? And unfortunately, at the time of his death, he hadn't taken care of any of her credit cards, either, which left her in a position where she couldn't even charge her way out of the mess.

One thing was for certain—she couldn't continue to live as she had. She plopped back on her bed and contemplated her ceiling and came to the only conclusion she could—it was time to sell off everything she had of value, *before* the bank came and claimed it.

Then she could create a whole new life for herself. A lot less luxurious life, but she could handle that. Already, she'd discovered some of the joy of taking care of herself. For one thing, her new friends—Vince, Andy, Tim, even

Amy—they were all *real* friends. They wouldn't desert her because she wasn't heir to a fortune. They couldn't care less, they just *liked* her.

Her.

That was a new and welcome surprise.

They liked her for being Caitlin, not for where Caitlin could take them.

It was possible that way down deep, she'd been waiting for this, wishing for the chance to prove to herself she could make it on her own, without any help.

Seemed she was about to get her wish.

DARN IT, but she was late again.

"You *had* to stop to talk to that lost homeless lady," Caitlin berated herself as she raced down the street, her purse flapping behind her. "Had to worry about her instead of yourself and your job and your undoubtedly furious boss."

Huffing and puffing, she dashed into the office building that housed CompuSoft. Because her lungs were threatening to explode right out of her chest, she sagged against the wall in the downstairs reception area, trying to catch her breath.

"Close to the quarter-century mark," she muttered out loud, "and already in pathetic shape."

"Caitlin? You okay?"

Holding a hand to her chest, she turned to face a startled Vince, who had one of Amy's scrumptious doughnuts in his hand.

Her mouth started to water. She'd missed breakfast again.

Amy looked concerned, too, and without a word she poured Caitlin some water, which Caitlin gratefully took. "I…will be fine…in just a…sec."

Vince grinned and gave her a slow once-over. "If you're trying to get in shape, you're too late. You already are."

"Well, I appreciate that," she gasped. "But I'm not…doing this to myself on purpose, believe me. I hate exercise." Wryly, she glanced down at her running shoes, then kicked them off. Reaching into her shoulder bag, she pulled out her high-heeled sandals. She'd been doing this every morning, changing downstairs while visiting with Amy, before going to the second floor and facing Joe.

"Why were you running?" Vince held out his arm so that she could use it to keep her balance while she fastened her sandals.

She grabbed on to him, feeling the bulge of muscle, the fine silk of his shirt beneath her fingers. Vince, unlike Tim, Andy and even Joe, never wore jeans to work. He was always dressed impeccably, and today was no different. The deep blue of his shirt and trousers matched his dark sapphire eyes perfectly and toned down the brilliance of his hair.

He waited, his eyes laughing down into hers. "Was that a tough question?"

"I'm sorry," she said quickly, flushing when

she realized he thought she'd been staring at him in frank appreciation. She *did* appreciate him, just not in the way he thought.

She appreciated his friendship, because at this point in her life friendship was a new and exciting gift. Somehow, though, she knew Vince wouldn't take it in the flattering light she meant it. "I was running because I'm late. As usual. The bus—"

"Where's your car?"

"It's gone," she said as cheerfully as she could with a lump the size of a regulation football stuck in her throat.

She missed her Beemer!

"You take the bus in from the beach every day?" he asked incredulously. "That's an awful commute, Caitlin."

"It's not so bad." What was awful was the kind and sincere horror in his voice at what she had to go through to get to work. "But the bus never seems to come on time. They say seven-fifteen, but they don't really mean it. Now I finally get the meaning—" she huffed as she worked her second sandal on "—when they say *Californian* time."

Vince laughed as he gently supported her. "Don't worry—I'll tell Joe it was my fault."

"*Your* fault," she repeated. "How on earth could my tardiness be *your* fault—" She broke off as she realized exactly what Joe would think when Vince told him that.

Vince laughed again when she flushed and said, *"Oh."*

"Come on," he said, tugging her to the elevator. "It'll be fun. He's so entertaining when he's furious."

While Caitlin knew darn well Joe didn't want her for himself, she instinctively knew how he would react if one of his techs wanted her. "Just yesterday, when Tim was going to program the clock to swear out loud on the hour, you reminded him how much pressure Joe was under right now."

"So?"

"So why tease him now? He's still under pressure. He might explode."

Vince pushed the button for their floor and grinned down at her. "Yeah. Think how much fun this is going to be."

"Vince—"

He pulled her into the elevator, but just as the door started to close, an elegant, leather-clad foot stopped it.

"Wait!" a female voice cried, and Vince pressed the open-door button.

Caitlin watched as the tall, willowy, incredibly beautiful woman stepped gracefully into the elevator and smiled familiarly at Vince. "Thanks, hon." Her long limbs moved fluidly as she settled herself. Her ankle-length white sheath was striking against her dark skin.

Now, that's a body, Caitlin thought enviously. All lean and toned—no extra curves there! She was just thinking how lovely the waist-length, heavy sable hair was when the woman turned to her…and frowned.

Caitlin recognized that frown, *and* its disapproval.

Joe gave it to her all the time. She stiffened in automatic response.

"This is Darla," Vince told her. "She's the accountant in the building. And Darla, this is Caitlin. Our secretary."

Caitlin smiled, but it wasn't her usual genuine, shining one because she felt suddenly drained.

"Are you enjoying the work?" Darla asked coolly.

"It's interesting."

Darla's expression opened up a bit, surprised. "You mean, he's letting you do something other than answer phones?"

Not that *he* knows, Caitlin thought. "Well…let's just say we're working on it."

"Ah." Darla's mouth curved. "Well, at least you made it past the two-day mark. No one else has."

"What a surprise that is."

Darla did smile then, a genuine one. "I see you're not enamored. That's good. Maybe you have a shot at making it in that office before he eats you alive."

"Enamored?" Because the thought was so ridiculous, Caitlin laughed.

"He's not an easy man," Darla agreed. "As you've obviously noticed."

"I've noticed."

"But he's a good one."

Yes. And also hard, tough, unforgiving and sexy as hell. "He's a good man," she agreed quietly, because it was the truth.

"You know…" Darla tipped her head to study Caitlin carefully. "You're *much* more than Barbie meets *Baywatch*. I'll have to tell Joe I was wrong about you."

"Barbie meets—" Caitlin sputtered, whipped her head to glare at Vince when he burst out laughing at her expression.

The elevator stopped. Darla smiled, and this time it was warm and genuine. "Bye, Caitlin. Good luck today. Or maybe I should wish Joe good luck. I have a feeling he's going to need it."

Caitlin wished she'd left her tennis shoes on, because for the first time in her life she felt like running. She wanted to race directly to Joe and tell him what she thought of him and his accountant.

"Caitlin, wait," Vince called out, trying to keep up with her as she made her way down the hallway.

"I don't think so." She kept going, driven by a need to give Joseph Brownley a piece of her mind. A big piece. A great big huge piece that would knock him flat on his far too gorgeous butt.

Unfortunately for Tim and Andy, they happened to be lurking around her desk when Caitlin stormed in. Twin smiles greeted her, only to die at the murderous expression on her face.

"What's wrong?" Andy asked quickly.

Vince grimaced. "She just met Darla...."

"Tell me," she said evenly, tossing her purse to the floor by her desk and placing her hands on her hips. She blew a strand of hair away from her face. "What did the other secretaries look like?"

In unison, the twins turned to Vince, confused. Vince sighed and shook his head.

"Oh, come on, guys," she encouraged. "*Think.* You remember, the ones who quit?" Her voice held a poisonous mixture of sweet smile and deadly tone. "Were they...pretty?"

"Not like you," Andy said loyally, and Tim shook his head vigorously.

"Darla didn't mean it," Vince said quietly to her, touching her arm, his eyes deep with concern and regret.

"No? But I'll bet Joe did." She dragged in a deep breath, stunned to find herself so upset.

"Caitlin, what's the matter?" Andy asked. "*What* didn't Darla mean?"

All three of them were looking at her in concern. Not one of them was on the verge of laughter. They really cared, Caitlin realized with a burst of surprise and warmth. They cared that she was upset, and they didn't find it funny. It went a long way toward soothing her. "Nothing," she said, forcing a smile. "It wasn't important."

"It was if it hurt you." Tim came closer, peering into her face. "Darla's really pretty great, but she does like a good joke. What did she say?"

Caitlin dropped her gaze from his, feeling a little silly. "Something about Barbie meets *Baywatch*," she muttered.

His eyes widened. He bit his lip, which Caitlin would have sworn was so he couldn't laugh. Next to her, Andy made a suspicious noise, something like a strangled hyena. In a Joe-like move, Vince closed his eyes.

"Oh, stop it," she said, biting back her own smile. "It really wasn't so funny a minute ago."

"You know it's not exactly a put-down," Vince offered in his boss's defense. "Most women would kill to be described that way." His eyes stayed on hers. "And no offense, but you really do look every bit as good as Barbie, or any one of those women on *Baywatch* for that matter."

"Really?" She let her gaze run over his own well-proportioned body. "How would *you* feel to be known as…oh, I don't know. How about Fabio meets G.I. Joe?"

Vince grinned. *"Fabio?"* He flexed his muscles. "Cool."

Caitlin rolled her eyes and gave up. "Oh, never mind." She shooed them all back to their offices and went to the small kitchen. Quietly, efficiently, she started the new coffeemaker, because of course it was empty. She waited impatiently until the coffee began to drip into the pot.

Filling a mug to the top with the steaming brew, she went back into the hall and contemplated the closed door to Mr. Gorgeous Butt's office.

She knocked.

"Go away."

She smiled and walked in.

Joe didn't even waste a scowl on her, but sat hunched over his computer, his fingers whirling away on the keyboard. "Back off or die," he muttered without much heat. "And you're late. Again."

Suddenly he froze. Then he lifted his head and sniffed. "Coffee? *Real* coffee?"

"As opposed to fake?" she asked sweetly, holding the mug just out of his reach. He stood so he could outreach her.

He'd gone all out today, wearing a light blue shirt instead of his usual black. His jeans, faded from wear, fit his long, lean limbs like a glove. When his fingers brushed hers, shocking her with that ever present electricity that ran between them, she gave over the mug.

Clearly unaffected, he sipped gratefully, then let out a huge sigh. "Thanks."

She lifted a brow. "Thanks? *Thanks*? Did you actually thank me? That can't be—you're never polite."

He looked insulted. "I'm plenty polite."

"Really?"

"Of course I am. I'm diplomatic, too."

Caitlin pretended to contemplate this while she walked the length of his office. Turning back to him, she asked, "Is it *polite* to discuss your employees with friends? Is it *diplomatic* to laugh at them, about them, behind their back?"

"What are you talking about?"

"Is it considered politically correct to resort to name-calling, especially before you even really know that employee?"

"What the hell are you talking about?"

"Does 'Barbie meets *Baywatch*' mean anything to you?"

His mouth opened a bit. "Oh," he said, his face unreadable. "You've...met Darla."

She waited for more, but he said nothing else. "That's *all* you have to say?"

He shrugged. "If it matters, you don't look like a model in the least to me."

"Gee, thanks," she said, feeling inexplicably flattened. The first man in the universe who didn't think she was pretty, and this depressed her?

She was an idiot.

"You have too much..." He waved his hand wildly, gesturing to her body, under the mistaken impression she wanted a detailed analysis of her body type. "Everything. Yeah, that's it. You have far too much *everything*."

"Hmm." The warning in her voice might have deterred another man, a normal man, but then again, Joe was anything but *normal*.

"And your hair isn't like Barbie's at all," he offered. "It's short, for one thing."

"I see."

"As for *Baywatch*..." He shrugged. "I've never seen the show, but it's supposedly got those tight red bathing suits, and I can't see you in one of those, either."

"You can't? Too much 'everything' to fit into one of them, huh?"

"Come on, princess, I can't be telling you anything you don't already know."

"*I'm not a princess.*" Each word was enunciated, and spoken very quietly. "If I were, do you think I'd be working for pennies for you?"

Suddenly wary, he looked at her, as if just realizing she wasn't taking this in quite the same lighthearted tone he'd meant it. "Caitlin—"

"Set down your coffee, Joe," she said evenly.

He did. "Why?"

"Because I'm going to act like a princess and have a temper tantrum. I don't want you to burn yourself." She swiped at the neat stack of papers on his desk, knocking them to the floor. She reached for another stack, getting into the spirit.

Laughing, he grabbed her hand and held it tight in a fist that might as well have been steel. "What was that for? Wait!"

But she simply switched tactics and tried to evade him. "Don't...patronize me," she demanded. "Don't talk about me behind my back, and *don't*..." She let out a huff of steam when he grabbed her, roaring with laughter.

Seeing red, she fought him. "Let me go!" she demanded, puffing and gasping for air as she fought.

With surprising speed and agile strength, he managed to wrap both arms around her and haul her close, pressing her now useless limbs against his own.

At the contact, she went utterly still.

So did Joe.

In the silence, their rough breathing sounded abnormally loud.

And arousing.

"Are we fighting," he wondered in a suddenly low, husky voice, all traces of humor gone as he stared down into her uplifted face, "or are we playing?"

"I...I don't know."

7

"I THOUGHT we were fighting." Caitlin stared at Joe with her huge, glowing eyes. She wiggled a bit, pressing all those terrific curves to him and causing interesting things to happen to his insides. And outsides. "But now...I've lost track."

Joe had, too. His heart was pounding, his body responding to the tight, erotic hold he had on her. She stared at his mouth, only inches from hers. Then hers opened slightly and he nearly moaned.

"Joe."

"This is crazy," he muttered.

"Yeah. Insane." But she tipped her torso up to his, and her round breasts pressed into his chest.

He was lost.

"Stop me," he begged, dipping his head down so he could slide his lips over her jaw. He nipped at the corner of her delicious mouth. "Stop me, Caitlin."

She skimmed her hands beneath his shirt to streak across his bare back, and caught the lobe of his ear between her teeth. His eyes crossed with lust, and the ball of heat he'd been stoking in his gut for days kindled.

"I...don't think I want to stop you." She sounded breathless. Confused. Aroused.

"So we're both crazy. Hell." And he kissed her.

Her fingers dug into his shoulders as the ball of heat erupted into fire. The soft, needy whimper that escaped her undid him, and he dragged her closer, lifting her up against him so that he could get better access to those lips and what lay beyond them. Under his fingers, her skin felt so soft, so warm, so inviting, he became dizzy with it.

So did Caitlin.

Passion.

Desire. She hadn't realized just one kiss could provoke it. Demand it. He surrounded her with his strength, his hunger. This was what she'd been missing. *This.* And she wanted more.

Joe stroked his fingers down her neck, discovered the pulse drumming at the base of her throat. Unable to resist, he bent his head to explore it with his mouth. She tasted like heaven, all sweet, melting irresistibility. Bringing his mouth back to hers, he swallowed her gasp as he trailed his fingers across the soft, slick silk of her snug-fitting blouse. He cupped her breasts, running his thumbs over their tight peaks. Gasping, she arched her body into his.

He had to see her eyes, had to know if she felt half of what he did. He was breathless when he lifted his head to look into her face. At the sudden loss of his warm lips, Caitlin protested wordlessly by fisting her hands in his hair and capturing his mouth again.

He understood, for he also feared he might never get enough. And he'd seen the cloudy desire in her eyes, mirroring his own. Her mouth opened to his, hot and hungry, and the room was filled with their sounds of pleasure... Then the sound of the office door opening.

Caitlin jerked in his arms. Still holding her, Joe lifted his head, prepared to bite someone's— anyone's—head off.

But whoever had opened the door had already retreated, leaving a conspicuously empty doorway.

Joe forced himself to look into Caitlin's eyes, prepared for the regret and the recriminations he deserved, but there were none.

Arms still looped around his neck, she smiled at him. A full, dazzling, vivid smile that did funny things to his heart and made his throat tighten uncomfortably.

There was an excellent explanation for what was happening, he assured himself—*insanity*. It was all he could come up with to account for holding this wild, unstable, unpredictable, irritating-as-hell woman in his arms. For kissing her until they'd both lost their senses.

"I don't suppose," she said softly, threading her fingers through his hair, making him want to purr with satisfaction at just her light touch, "you'd like to try that again."

"Caitlin." It wasn't possible. They shouldn't

have indulged in the first place. Slowly, with some regret, he reached up and unhooked her arms from around his neck.

"I guess not," she said, still sounding cheerful, and she backed up a step, which allowed him to see into those incredible brown eyes.

They were filled with hurt. Silently calling himself every name he could think of, he reached for her, but she danced back. "No." She shook her head and scooted around his chair, holding it between them like a shield. "No pity embraces, okay? You kissed me, you're regretting it, let's just let it go at that."

"I don't pity you," he said gruffly. "You're far too maddening for that."

"Another compliment." She pressed a hand to her chest and batted her lashes at him. "You really must stop—it'll go to my head."

"This is a business," he said carefully. "And I don't mix business with pleasure."

"Well, you've got a funny way of showing it, but don't worry, boss, I won't forget who signs the paychecks." Caitlin swallowed her hurt. "And if it makes you feel any better, I can not like you very much and still enjoy kissing you."

"I meant," he said tightly, his probing gaze pinning her to the spot, "that this...this—"

"Yes? This what, Joe? Relationship? No, that would be too much, wouldn't it."

"What do you want from me?"

His expression wasn't grim or angry; those

she could have easily resisted. He seemed...
genuinely baffled. And scared.

That stopped her as nothing else could have.
He was nervous and unsettled. The big, restless,
ill-tempered, bullheaded man was backpedaling
as fast as he could because she terrified him.
"That's the funny thing here, Joe. I don't want
anything from you."

"Women always do."

"Is that right?" She studied him thoughtfully.
"Yeah, I can see that might be a problem. Gorgeous, smart...and such a charming bedside
manner. How ever do you fight them all off?"

When he took another step toward her, scowling, her heart raced, but not from fear. Damn
him, he'd done the impossible. He'd made her
want him and now he was regretting it. She
could really hate him for that. But she knew if he
so much as touched her, she'd fling herself into
those very capable arms.

She backed to the door, grabbed the jamb for
balance and sent him a smile, though it wavered. "You know what? Never mind this
whole thing. I've got work."

"Wait." He paused, drew a ragged breath.
"I'm sorry," he said in that unbearably sexy
voice that was now filled with tenderness and
affection—two emotions she would never have
expected of him.

She turned away. "I'm not."

"Caitlin." She stopped, but didn't face him,

and when she heard his words, she was glad for it.

"This won't happen again. It can't."

"Okay."

"I mean it." His stern voice reminded her that she didn't like stern men who didn't see past her exterior to the woman beneath.

"Fine." Now, pride fierce and hot, she looked at him. "Remember that the next time you grab me close, Joe, okay? *Keep your lips to yourself.*"

THE CROWNING GLORY CAME late the next afternoon. Caitlin made the mistake of thinking about Joseph's kiss while working the new coffeemaker. She got herself so hot and bothered, she didn't pay attention to the strange crackling, sizzling sound coming from the outlet on the wall where the machine was plugged in.

The cord caught fire.

She figured the ensuing explosion was Joseph's final straw.

He came storming into the kitchen, eyes wild, hair standing up on end from where he'd plowed his fingers through it. "Again?" he yelled. "You're incredible! How does this happen to you? To *me*?" Unplugging the scorched, blown-up unit from the wall, he hissed at the heat. Now that there was coffee from ceiling to floor, there were no more flames.

Just that scorched-coffee smell.

With one swift look at the calamity around him, he went straight to her.

Caitlin couldn't bring herself to look at him, but he lifted her chin with his fingers. "You okay?" he asked, his voice low and serious.

She nodded, sure she'd never felt so stupid in all her life.

"You're sure?" He turned her face from side to side, inspecting her thoroughly. She nodded again.

"Good." He drew a deep breath and glanced at the mess around them. "Then I can yell at you and not feel bad."

"Maybe I'm not so okay after all," she decided, but he didn't find her humorous in the least.

Tim, Andy and Vince appeared in the doorway, eyes wide, faces grim.

"In fact," she said urgently, "I'm critically injured. Probably going to die."

"She's kidding," Joe told them. "I'll handle this." To underscore his point, he shut the door in their faces. The room suddenly shrank.

"I can't work like this," he said, far too quietly. "If I don't get some peace soon, Caitlin, I'll blow up. Just like the coffeemaker."

What could she say—she had no idea what she'd done wrong, other than be born. Man, he had such great, wide shoulders—perfect for setting her head down on. They were so strong, so durable. She could lean there and cry it all out— her fears for her future…how she was beginning to feel for him…that she didn't want to be alone anymore. She thought maybe he could feel the same way about her if he tried really hard and overlooked all the little things that drove him crazy....

"I'm sorry. I really do know how to make coffee, honest."

"I'm so close to finishing this program. I'm so damn close, and you keep distracting me, driving me insane. Do you do it on purpose?"

"No, it's just a special talent of mine." But she thought it only fair he take half the blame for the coffeemaker thing. It had been *his* lips, *his* touch, *his everything* that had distracted her in the first place; otherwise she would have noticed the fire.

He paced the small kitchen, his sneakers making squishy noises in the coffee. He looked huge. Powerful. Very dangerous. "I thought I could do this—I swear I did. Dammit, I wanted to for Edmund."

Her heart lodged in her throat. "What are you saying?"

"That I can't do this anymore. I just can't." With a sound of disbelief, he gestured around him. "Look at this, Caitlin. Did you know we've been here for years and never once has that damn thing exploded? You've done it twice now." In disgust, he lifted a foot, and it came loose from the linoleum with a loud pop. "We've never even had to mop before you came here."

"I don't think that's necessarily something to be proud of. A good cleaning never hurt anything, Joe."

"Well it's gotten two cleanings in four days! There are more important things to be doing, dammit!"

"And I'd be happy to be doing them, but you don't trust me!"

"Trust you! You can't even work a coffee-maker!"

"All right, fine!" she yelled back, her hands on her hips. "But we all make mistakes. You don't see me flinging yours in *your* face."

"Because I haven't made any," he shouted, matching her tone as they stood nose to nose raging at each other.

"You make me so—"

The doorway to the kitchen was suddenly filled with curious, frantic techs.

"Get out!" Joe reached over and slammed the door.

"That wasn't nice." Caitlin lifted her chin. "They're probably just wondering what you're hollering about."

"They're used to it, believe me," Joe assured her. He let out a slow breath. "And you're changing the subject. I make you so...what? So mad?"

So horny. The thought came unbidden, but it didn't quite apply here. "Yes! Mad and irritated and frustrated and anxiety ridden."

"Is that all?"

"You also infuriate me."

"That's the same as mad."

"It's mad multiplied."

"My point exactly." He nodded, quite calm now. "We drive each other crazy, so—"

"I never said you drove me crazy."

He sighed and closed his eyes, looking so defeated, she wanted to hug him. *Hug him?*

Maybe *she* was crazy.

"You're skirting around the real issue."

"Of course I am," she snapped. "You're trying to fire me and pretend it has nothing to do with what happened earlier in your office. Which is a crock!"

A knock came at the door, followed by Tim's hesitant voice. "Guys? Everything all right in there?"

"It would be if you would go back to your office and do your job!" Joe roared at the closed door.

"There's no need to yell at him—he's just being sweet," Caitlin proclaimed, nearly yelling herself. She never raised her voice, so it was startling to realize how good it felt. So exhilarating. So freeing. "And no need to shout at me, either. It's yourself you're so mad at."

Joe let out a short laugh and glanced around him at the coffee mess. "How in the hell do you figure that?"

"*You* kissed *me*," she reminded him, jabbing a finger to his chest. "And you liked it, Joe."

"Joe? Caitlin?" This time it was Andy, and the knob turned. Bravely, he pushed open the door. "You're going to bring the place down. What's going on?"

"Nothing!" they shouted in unison.

"If you're trying to fire her," Vince said flatly, peeking around Andy. "Forget it. We took a vote. She stays."

"It's *my* vote that counts," Joe said. He'd made a living out of calling the shots; retreat didn't come naturally. He met Caitlin's fathomless dark eyes and couldn't, for the life of him, look away.

Time stopped and inexplicably he couldn't remember why he was so mad.

As if she sensed that, her lips curved softly.

His heart tipped. Just tipped right over and broke a little. Yeah, he wanted her, but even worse, he *needed* her. Not an easy admission, even to himself. Never losing eye contact, he said, "Fine. Dammit. She stays. You're all crazy." It threw him to see her smile fully now. "What's so damn amusing?" he demanded.

"You are." She said this sweetly and full of such warmth and affection that for a minute he couldn't breathe, much less speak. "You think you're so tough," she added softly. Moving close, she reached up and cupped his cheek.

At the unexpected contact, he flinched. "I *am* tough."

She shook her head, still smiling. Her eyes glowed. "You're a big softie, Joe Brownley."

Vince laughed from the doorway. "Yeah. A big softie. Ask him for a raise, Caitlin. Let's see just how soft."

Joe shifted uncomfortably. He wasn't soft at

all, but hard as a rock at just her touch. "Get out of here, guys. Caitlin and I have things to discuss."

"Things?" Andy lifted a brow curiously. "What things?"

"Yeah, what things?" Tim wanted to know, ignoring the order to leave. They leaned against the doorjamb, comfortable. Completely uncowed by Joseph's glare.

So much for tough. "Get out," he repeated firmly, keeping his gaze on Caitlin.

He didn't hear anyone budge. Not until Caitlin turned to them with that endearing smile, the one that could make a grown man beg, and said in her light, gentle voice, "It's all right. We'll try to keep it down."

Joe watched, stunned, as Tim and Andy smiled back at Caitlin dopily, completely entranced, and then did as she asked. Vince left, too, silently.

When they were alone, he said, "That's amazing. The way you twist everyone around that little pinkie of yours."

"What things do we have to discuss, Joe?"

"Rules, princess. Rules."

"Ah." She nodded. "Those rules again."

He ran his gaze over her lush, curvy body, and his fingers itched to explore. "Apparently, you've forgotten them."

"Gee, I guess we're back to the topic of my clothes."

They both looked at her choice for the day—

narrow denim skirt unbuttoned from ankle to well above the knee, topped with a tight, siren-red, ribbed cotton top.

He cleared his throat. "I told you we were conservative around here."

"No, you said I should wear *more*. Well, my skirt goes practically to the floor." She lifted her foot and wiggled her bright red sandal, exposing a terrific looking leg to midthigh. "I'm trying to fit in with the norm around here."

"Which is?"

"Casual." Caitlin lifted her gaze up to his and found his beautiful eyes filled with equal parts heat and annoyance. *Perfect*. Now their moods matched. "What do you think?"

He curled an arm around her waist, still annoyed. Still hot. He dragged her closer. "I think you're courting disaster."

"Am I?" she whispered, their lips nearly touching as she strained against him on tiptoe. Gently, she framed his face, marveling at herself. Never in her life had she made a move on a man; now she couldn't seem to stop. "This isn't a disaster. This is the rescue."

"Rescue?" His voice, thick and sexy, nearly had her dissolving in a boneless heap.

"Yeah." She kissed the corner of his mouth, loving the feel of his warm and solid body against hers. "You're something. All those hard muscles and that bad attitude. But you can't fool me, Joe. You care. You feel. And you need this." Her lips trailed over his clenched, slightly stubbled jaw, and she lingered, suddenly overwhelmed by how he made her feel. She closed her eyes and kept going, expecting him to shove her away any second, but he didn't. Instead, he tilted his head, letting her have her way. "You need me," she whispered.

"You're pressing your luck, Caitlin." He didn't sound very steady or very tough at the moment.

"I don't think so."

Now he did move away, capturing her busy little hands in his. "You don't know me." In a gesture that tore at her, he lifted their joined hands to his lips. "You don't know the real me. All I care about, all I feel, is a passion for my work. There's not room for anything else."

"Or *anyone* else?"

"I don't want anyone in my life." He stared at her hands resting in his. "I really don't."

It was hard to reconcile this man with the abrupt, gruff one that she usually saw. Both were passionate, fierce, intelligent. But this Joe...*this* one she could really like. She told him so.

He let her hands go. "I don't want you to like me."

"You can control your computers, Joe," she said softly. "But you can't control me."

"I *can* control this," he contradicted her. "I can and I will. Because it would be a mistake, Caitlin. We would be a huge mistake. You'd get hurt, and I..."

"Yes?" she wondered with patience. "You'd what? You'd maybe get hurt, too? Well, isn't that what life's all about?"

"Dammit, we're not talking about me. We're talking about you, and how you'd feel when it was over. Afterward."

Now she laughed, though without a lot of humor. "I never said I wanted you, Joe."

"You do."

She let out a genuine chuckle. "Okay, maybe I do. But don't panic—it's just physical. Pure and simple. I'd be crazy to want more with you."

But she *was* crazy, she thought. And she did want more, much more. She sidled up close, batted her lashes at him flirtatiously. "Come on, Joe. Let's play."

"No. No way." He nearly ran to the door.

Just before he shut it, she called out, "So can I have the raise?"

8

CAITLIN SPENT THE WEEKEND in a strange state of awareness. Friday night, she went dancing with Amy, where they met Tim and Andy and had a great time.

Caitlin realized how much more these friends meant to her than any others she'd ever had.

Things had changed for her, she decided. They'd changed with her father's death, with her new job. Once she'd lived her life casually, without thought to past or future, but no longer.

For the first time, she had people in her life who cared about the *real* Caitlin, not the spoiled rich one.

Everything else—her financial woes, her worries of what would happen to her future—paled in comparison to that.

Somehow, in the past few months, priorities had shifted.

Now when she looked in the mirror, she no longer saw a pampered woman, but one who lived, laughed, cared....

One who loved.

BY MONDAY CAITLIN WAS already out of money—again—and very tired of taking the bus.

To cheer herself up, she'd spent the last of her pocket change on doughnuts from Amy's stand. And while this endeared her greatly to Tim and Andy, she didn't imagine the scale in her bathroom was going to be so kind.

As she went into the small office kitchen, she glanced down at herself and rolled her eyes. Even wearing one of those bras that promised to control and contain—whatever the heck that meant—she still spilled out of whatever she wore. The flowered print dress she had on today dipped a little low in front, emphasizing the problem. And was it her fault her hips strained against the soft cotton? Nope, she decided, taking another bite of a huge chocolate-buttermilk roll. She might as well face it; she was never going to be a waif.

She studied her image in the front of the steel-door refrigerator. Wild blond bob. Red lips. Big eyes.

"You're beautiful, you know."

Jumping a little, she faced Vince. He shot her a little smile and gestured to the door she'd been using as a mirror. "You don't have to check," he said. "You are."

"I'd rather be known for my brains."

She said this with such disgust, he laughed. Then he sobered, stuck his hands into his trouser pockets and came closer. "I saw you and Joe on Friday. You know…in his office."

So *Vince* had interrupted their kiss!

"I don't want to see you get hurt," he said carefully. He squared his shoulders. He didn't have a single wrinkle. He was a man who appreciated fine clothes, a man with expensive tastes, a man after her own heart...and she didn't feel anything but a sisterly sort of affection.

What was wrong with her?

"I don't think it's a good idea for you to get involved with him."

Her brain, protesting the early hour, went on full alert. "Vince, he's your boss and your friend."

"I know. And I care about him very much." Vince met her gaze, and she knew he was genuinely sad. "But I care about you, too. Joseph's not easy on women, Caitlin. They come in and out of his life in a heartbeat. He rarely looks back."

Her unease grew. "We shouldn't be discussing this. It's not right."

"I care about you."

"But I'm a big girl," she said gently. She reached for his hand and squeezed. "You don't have to worry about me."

Everything about him was tense, even as he let out a little laugh. "I can't seem to help that."

"Well, seeing as there's little between me and your friend, except resentment and bad air, you don't have much to worry about."

"What I saw between the two of you was a lot more than bad air, Caitlin."

The kiss again. Well, it *had* been quite a kiss. Quite a very good kiss. The mother of all kisses. But it had meant nothing to Joe, which was what Vince was trying so gallantly to make sure she understood.

What she really understood was that Joe didn't *want* it to mean anything. That he wasn't comfortable with the intimacy, and she could understand that, as well. Neither was she.

What, she wondered, would Joe say if he knew she'd never experienced any sort of intimacy at all? It wasn't something she'd set out purposely to do, but she'd never found the right man. Somehow, it had been easy to resist the fast, rich, slick kind of guy her so-called friends had all hung out with. So now, despite her travels and exciting life-style, she was the oldest virgin in the Western Hemisphere. "I'm not going to get my heart broken over one kiss," she said, more weakly than she would have liked.

"I'm not doing a good job of warning you off him, am I?" Vince asked wryly.

"It's not your fault. I just never seem to learn what's good for me."

"I could be good for you," he said seriously.

"Oh, Vince."

He shook his head. "I'm sorry. I didn't mean to say that so soon." Softly, he touched her cheek, then walked away.

It didn't take long to get distracted. She took a call from the mortgage company for the condo her father hadn't left her. The by-the-book loan officer on the line was not impressed by her employment.

"Look, Ms. Taylor," he said in a voice bordering on nasty. "I do realize you have a job now, and apparently, you should be commended for that."

While Caitlin took his not so polite disdain, Joe walked by. He wore the customary faded jeans and T-shirt and was every bit as aloof and dangerously sexy as her dreams had assured her. With his heavily lidded eyes, that perpetual frown on his beautiful, scowling mouth and the rugged, muscled yet lean body, he looked every bit the hoodlum she imagined most mothers warned their daughters from.

But Caitlin didn't have a mother, and she doubted she would have listened to a mother's advice, anyway.

"Ms. Taylor," the mortgage officer said in her ear, "you can't expect this company to believe that you'll be able to make the payments, given your current salary. Not to mention how far behind you are already. I'm sorry, but the lock-out will take place on Friday evening, unless you come up with something else."

Lock out.

As in a huge padlock on her front door. She would have no place to go. "You're going to put me out on the street because you don't like my job?"

Joe, already across the office and halfway out the door, froze. Mortified, Caitlin lowered her voice and her head. "You can't do this," she told the jerk on the line. "You can't. My father—"

"Is dead," the man said bluntly. "And hasn't provided any means for paying the mortgage. You have no experience, no credits to your name and no viable means of providing us what is due, Ms. Taylor. You can't possibly blame us for this situation."

"What can I do to prove myself?" she asked, more than a little desperately. What had happened to her great life? To security? To a full stomach?

"Marry a rich man," he advised. "Quickly."

Floored, she hung up the phone and stared at it. She'd mistakenly thought her life was starting to be under control. But it wasn't even close, she realized, and dropped her head down to her desk.

What could she do?

Hand still on the office door, Joe stared at Caitlin's bowed head. Her full hair fell forward, exposing her pale, soft neck. She seemed small, vulnerable. Dammit, no. *No*, he told himself firmly.

You aren't going to worry about her.

But he let go of the door. Of their own accord, his feet took him to her desk. *Not his problem, absolutely not. Run, don't walk, to the nearest exit.* He perched a hip on the corner of her desk. *This has nothing, absolutely nothing, to do with his promise to Edmund. He'd gone over and above the call of duty so far. Anyone would think so.*

Anyone.

Instead of running, he heard himself say, "Caitlin? What's the matter?"

She jerked upright, flashed him a smile minus her usual megawattage and said with false cheer, "Nothing. Everything's perfect. Absolutely perfect."

"You're out of money."

"Nothing new."

"You're going to lose your place."

Her shoulders sagged. Her smile faded, and in its place came a disturbing helplessness. "It's not mine anyway."

So many emotions attacked him then, he couldn't think straight enough to sort them out from each other. But leading the way was guilt—guilt because Edmund had taken care of *him*, a punk kid with no future, yet he'd ignored his own daughter.

Despite how Joe felt about her, and how he *didn't* want to feel about her, she didn't deserve this. Anger bubbled. Anger at Edmund, anger for Caitlin and anger for himself at being left to deal with the mess.

He was distinctly uncomfortable cleaning up the messes other people made of their lives. He'd done it for his mother. He'd done it for his siblings. He'd done it for countless "friends" over the years who'd assumed that because of what he did for a living, he had an overabundance of money.

He didn't want to do it anymore. "I can help."

"No." Abruptly, Caitlin got up. "I need to walk," she said, slipping off her high-heeled sandals, replacing them with running shoes. Joe watched, fascinated and mesmerized, as her dress gaped and revealed soft, full, plump breasts rebelling against their constraints.

He was a jerk, he thought, staring down her dress when she was undergoing a crisis. He told himself this quite firmly. But he didn't—couldn't—stop looking.

When she grabbed her purse, he stopped her, pulled her back. Their thighs touched, but it no longer startled him to feel that inexplicable heat in his body. "Caitlin."

"No," she said quickly, trying to pull back. For once, her eyes didn't give her away. "No pity, remember?"

"I already told you," he said, lying only a little. "You're too prickly to feel sorry for."

"*I'm* prickly?" She laughed a little. "Right."

"Let me help," he said rashly, having no idea why the words popped out. "I want to."

"Why?"

Because already I can't stop thinking about you, and if I have to be worried on top of being distracted all to hell, I'll never get any peace. "Because you need it, dammit. Because your life is out of control, and you need help. I can supply that help. It's that simple."

She stared at him for a long moment, and he could have sworn she was waiting for something, something more. Her lovely dark eyes searched his, but he was still befuddled by the view she'd just given him, and by touching her, and he didn't know what else she could possibly want.

Finally, she turned away, but not before he saw her expression fall a little. "Thanks, but you've helped me enough. More than enough. Be back after lunch." She ran out the door.

He watched her go, remorse and lust gnawing equally at his gut.

CAITLIN FOUND HERSELF in the lobby, aimless.

"Hey, there."

She mustered a smile for Amy, who leaned over her food stand with a friendly smile that faded quickly enough at the expression on Caitlin's face.

"Uh oh, you've got *the face* on." Silently, Amy turned and grabbed a plate.

"What face?"

Amy bustled a moment, then turned with a heaping serving of cinnamon crumb cake. "The kind that is crying out for food. Preferably junk food, the more fattening the better."

Caitlin had to laugh. "Yeah, it's been that kinda day."

"Hmm, no kidding. Tell me."

"You tell me first," Caitlin urged, needing to hear about someone and something other than herself and her own troubles.

"Okay. My first customer of the day hits on me every morning despite the fact that I am madly in lust with the UPS guy. The UPS guy, who by the way is the most fab man on the planet, doesn't know I exist. My supplies were late and so was my alimony check, which means I am now late making my rent."

Caitlin hummed her complete understanding and nodded, encouraging Amy to continue because suddenly her own problems didn't seem so major.

"And if I'm late on my rent, it goes on my credit, and if I get bad credit, I can't buy a new car at the end of the year like I promised myself." She shrugged. "That about sums it up for today," Amy said. "Now you."

"Okay, my boss thinks I'm a helpless idiot. His best friend is falling for me and I don't want to hurt him. And...I think I'm falling for my boss."

"The one that thinks you're a helpless idiot."

"Yeah." She could have complained about the condo and the car. Or about her serious and frightening lack of money, but strangely enough, that stuff didn't matter as much.

"I like being my own boss," Amy said into their companionable silence. "And you couldn't hurt anyone if you tried, Caitlin. You're too kind."

"I— That's a very generous thing to say." Caitlin's throat tightened at the look of utter sincerity on Amy's face. "But you don't really know me."

"I think I do."

Hot tea came next, and Caitlin found herself being pampered by nothing but the best crumb cake she'd ever sampled and an even better friendship.

"You know," she mumbled around a huge, heavenly biteful, "I've been everywhere in this world. I've eaten at the most amazing places." She smiled at Amy's curious face. "But nothing has tasted as good as this."

"Well, I haven't been anywhere, other than Los Angeles, but that doesn't really count 'cause it's just in the next county over, you know?" Amy laughed completely unselfconsciously. "But I still know a good person when I meet one, Caitlin. Don't let them get you down. Life's too good, too short."

Caitlin stilled as the simple truth sunk in. "It is, isn't it?"

"You could get another job and drop all the problems in one shot."

Another truth, one that just a few days ago she would have thought an impossibility. But now she knew better. She knew she was smart enough to learn how to do whatever she wanted. "You know...you're right."

And she thought about it for the rest of the day. Imagined herself in another job, being appreciated, rewarded. Cared about.

Without Joe.

The tightness in her chest deepened and became an ache.

She was in bigger trouble than she ever imagined if the thought of being without Joe Brownley could so unsettle her.

CAITLIN DRAGGED HER FEET as she carried CompuSoft's bookkeeping to Darla's office, but it had to be done. Joe had told her. She had explained it wasn't necessary as she'd already reconciled his checkbook and had arranged his accounts receivables and payables.

He'd laughed. "And I'm the Pope."

She'd been disgusted, then furious at his assumption that she'd been joking, but now all she felt was hurt.

Amy's suggestion bounced around in her head.

Another job.

The prospect didn't seem quite so daunting anymore.

She found Darla in her office, laughing over something Tim had said. The phone rang, distracting her, for which Caitlin was thankful. She needed a moment to collect herself.

Tim smiled shyly as Darla dealt with her call, which went a long way toward boosting Caitlin's spirits. "You look really pretty today, Caitlin."

"Thanks." She forced a smile in return because Tim was probably the sweetest, most unassuming man she'd ever met. "Just tell Darla everything's there." *And done.* As she dropped the package on the desk, her gaze ran over a complicated spreadsheet opened there.

Darla hung up the phone and nodded politely to Caitlin, her eyes filled with curiosity. "Thanks. How's it going?"

"Perfect." But she was distracted. She pointed to the spreadsheet and spoke without thinking. "Did you know that this column is added up wrong? You've got the tens and hundreds column transposed."

Darla's dark gaze widened, then narrowed. "So that's why I didn't balance— How in the world did you figure that out so fast?"

"I just added them up." Caitlin held her breath at the look of bewildered shock on the woman's face. "Adding is a basic function you know. Even blondes can do it."

"This is more than just adding two plus two." Stunned, Darla stared at Tim. "Did you know she could do that?"

"No." Tim looked at Caitlin, *not* as though she were a freak as she expected, but with affection. "Cool. You're blond, beautiful *and* smart. Marry me?"

Darla snorted and shoved him out of the way. She opened the package Caitlin had brought. Her surprise was clear as she spread out the papers, realizing most of the work was complete. "This isn't Joseph's messy scrawl."

"No, it isn't."

Darla looked up. "Is it right?"

"You've seen me add."

Darla smiled slow and warm. "You know, *nothing* irritates me more than when someone sticks their nose in the air over the clinch cover on one of my favorite romance books. Do you know what I mean?"

"That I shouldn't make fun of your choice of reading material?"

Darla grasped Caitlin's hand, sent her a small, regretful smile. "I judged *you* by your cover, Caitlin. And I'm sorry for that. I hope you can forgive me."

There was no sign of the aloof woman Caitlin had first met on the elevator. Even that long, lean, perfect body of Darla's suddenly seemed less intimidating. "I did the same," Caitlin admitted, smiling in return. "Just forget it."

"I never forget a fellow number lover," Darla vowed. "When you get tired of Mr. Gorgeous Grump, come here. I'll hire you on the spot."

"I'm tired of Mr. Gorgeous Grump."

Darla laughed. "Well, then we've got a lot to talk about. You want to think about another job?"

"I already have."

Darla nodded approvingly. "Then let's do it."

THE PHONE RANG, and Joe automatically lifted the receiver, but his greeting died as Caitlin's mortgage officer introduced himself.

"You just missed Ms. Taylor," Joe said coolly. "But I'm her...attorney. How much does she owe and where do I send it?"

He took the information, silently calling himself every sort of fool. So he had this bizarre sense of protectiveness, so what?

If you had to become a bleeding heart, you idiot, you could have gotten a puppy. It would have been far cheaper.

Vince came in. "Where's the Huntley contract?"

"I had that one out last week. It should be…hell." With dread, he looked down at the desk that was now Caitlin's. It was cleared off. So was the floor, he realized with growing horror. "I had it here. I used to have lot of files here. Oh, God." Sick, he looked up. "I don't see any files here, Vince."

Vince bit his lip.

"Tell me she didn't file," he urged. "Please. Tell me she's just been sitting here answering phones, blowing up coffee machines and looking pretty."

"Well…"

With one short, concise oath, Joe stood. "Where?" he said quietly, and Vince pointed to the series of filing cabinets against the wall. "She told me the other day she'd been doing a little at a time. She, uh…revamped your system for you."

"Oh, great." Knowing Caitlin, things could be anywhere. Individual contracts could have been grouped and filed away under *N* for "Nasty-Looking Documents." Detailed software instructions, which tended to look like maps, could have been filed under anything from *D* for "Directions," to *L* for "Looks like Latin to me."

"I'm going to have to kill her."

Vince sighed and moved toward the files. "No. Then I'd have to kill you. Too messy, Joe."

Unreasonable jealousy reared up and smacked him, hard. She'd made instant friends with these guys. Real friends. They were already as loyal to her as they were to him, maybe more. Joe had never in his life made an instant friend, and he was afraid that said something about him. Something he didn't like.

She was just a woman, he reminded himself. One woman. And while he knew it was a rotten, unfair generalization, he'd found that most women were manipulators. That had always been fine with him, since he'd never wanted one for more than the usual quick fling.

But now things were different. He didn't want a quick fling with Caitlin. All he wanted was his work. Oh, man, he couldn't lie to himself. He *did* want a quick, hard fling, and that really got him. This was his *work*, dammit. Work and pleasure did not mix!

Tim and Andy came in, and when they found out what Caitlin had done, they quickly offered to help.

"Keep in mind," Andy said, flipping through the first drawer, "if you fire her now, we'll go back to answering our own phones, and you'll get even less done. Think of your program, Joe.

The one you're almost done with. Our future, man. Just remember."

"Yeah, our future." Joseph's mouth tightened. Since Caitlin had joined them, he'd accomplished little toward that goal. What made it worse, he couldn't put all the blame at her feet.

For some reason, when he sat at his computer, he now spent a good amount of time just staring at it, seeing a certain brown-eyed, sweet-smiling, drop-dead-gorgeous blonde. Thinking. Wishing. Hoping. And it annoyed him.

The files were...perfect. As were in the As. Bs in the Bs. And so on. The Huntley file was with the Hs. It was a miracle.

And he was a jerk.

"She did a good job," Vince noted casually.

"But...I told her to answer phones." Baffled now, he looked around. He hardly recognized his surroundings; everything looked so good, so clean. So...uncluttered.

"She's done much more than just answer phones," Vince said, somewhat accusingly. "She's *made* this place, Joe. You should tell her. Thank her."

That Vince was right didn't help, but how to explain what he'd known all along? Caitlin could drive him off the brink. She was sexy, and yes, dammit, smarter than he wanted to admit.

This, he told himself harshly, was what happened when he went against his better judgment. He hadn't wanted to work with her. Had tried to find a way out of it. But short of breaking his promise to a man who'd meant everything to him, he hadn't found a way.

"Here's the general ledger that Darla called about. It's right here, in the accounting stuff, just where it should be."

Joe groaned, knowing the ledger that Darla had been asking for was two weeks overdue, and one thing Darla wasn't, was patient. He'd had it on the front desk, but apparently his efficient secretary had taken care of it for him.

He would have to face Darla, too.

The phone rang again, this time from a slimy used-car salesman Joe wouldn't have turned his back on. When he realized that Caitlin had called this guy, looking for a used car she could afford, his stomach actually cramped. She'd lost her car.

Dammit, Edmund. *Why?*

He hung up on the sales-scum, then promptly took another call. It was the building electrician. The wiring in his kitchen was faulty.

Faulty.

Joe grit his teeth as he listened to the man explain how the entire kitchen could have gone up in flames instead of just blowing up the coffeemaker.

It hadn't been Caitlin's fault—neither time.

He was rotten to the core.

BY THE END of the week, Joe was losing it. Really losing it. For days, he'd been making a new career out of staring at his computer. Sometimes, for variety, he swore at it.

But the final straw came on Friday.

Caitlin didn't show.

He was in his office with Darla when Vince informed him that Caitlin wasn't coming in.

"Good, maybe I'll get something done for a change," Joe said with bright relief for Darla's and Vince's benefit. Meanwhile, his insides sank. A weekend was coming up. Now he wouldn't catch a glimpse of her for three days. Not one look at those huge, haunting brown eyes. Not one peek at her full red mouth that he knew damn well was more addicting than any drug. Not to mention her other notable...parts.

Worse, he'd have no one to spar with. Oh, he could pick on any of the techs. Or Darla. All of them could be counted on to give as good as they got. Except Tim, who usually just pouted.

But no one gave him what Caitlin did. A run for his money. A kick start to a whirl of emotional adrenaline he hadn't experienced in far too long, which itself was good enough reason to stay clear of her. He didn't need to feel that attachment. Didn't want to.

Nope. In fact, he should be ecstatic that she wasn't coming in, and his temper stirred when he realized he wasn't even close. "Is she sick?"

"No." Vince moved to the door. "She's moving tomorrow and needs to do some stuff."

"*What?*"

"She didn't tell you?"

To the amusement of both Darla and Vince, Joseph yanked up the phone and called her. "Why didn't you tell me you were moving?" he demanded when he got her on the line.

"What does that matter?" came her surprisingly weary voice. "But I'm sorry about today. I'll be there Monday."

She hung up on him.

The nerve. No one had ever— "Vince," he barked as his poor tech was trying to escape. "She's moving? By herself?"

"Yeah."

He'd paid the mortgage, dammit!

"I told her I'd come tonight to help her pack. She didn't want me to, but I'm going anyway." He hesitated. "Actually, she sounded poorly. I think I'll just go now."

Joe swore again. Darla lifted her brows and glanced at him. The knowing light in her eyes was hard to take.

"Fine," he said stiffly to Vince. No problem, he was fine with it.

Vince left and Darla smiled. "Okay," she drawled. "Where were we? The expenses, I believe." She lifted her pencil and smiled at him.

"Yeah. The expenses." He tried to concentrate. He didn't want to think about the woman who'd set his world upside down with one sweet smile and a little chaos. Because then he'd have to admit that Caitlin's presence wasn't so much an intrusion as a breath of fresh air. That having her around didn't disrupt him nearly as much as his feelings for her.

"We agreed that you were going to capital-ize—"

And his feelings for her were driving him crazy. "I just can't."

"Okay." Darla shrugged. "I'll talk you into the capitalization thing later." She tapped the spreadsheet. "About the revenue."

"No."

"No?"

"I can't." His head dropped with a loud thunk to his desk. "This is out of control."

"Not you," she said with amusement. "Not the king of all control. Smooth, unruffled computer whiz Joe Brownley, paving the way for the offices of the future..."

"Darla?" His voice was muffled against the wood of his desk.

"Hmm?"

"Shut up."

"I'd love to, darling," she said smoothly, sympathetically rubbing his back, "but I need your tax info."

"Take it," he begged. "I need some peace."

"Yeah?" She pondered this as she worked on the knots of his shoulders. "Been rough, huh?"

"Worse."

"Then I guess now is not the time to tell you that Caitlin did most of the grunt work on this accounting."

He lifted his head. "What?"

"She's a little math wizard, Joe."

"She's a..." He closed his eyes. "I'm such an ass."

"Undoubtedly," she agreed. "But stop sweating the small stuff." She tugged him back up. "And get to the meat of it." She tapped the paperwork in front of them. "Tax time, buddy."

But all he could think was that Caitlin had sounded so sad. So alone. And she'd done his accounting while he'd ribbed her intelligence, mocked her at every turn.

"Let's get a move on." Darla looked at him, her eyes sparkling with humor. "Unless, of course, there's something else—or *somewhere* else—you need to be?"

Vince is probably nearly there. "Just get on with it," he urged, needing to be sidetracked. Vince was perfect for her. Perfect.

"Okay." Darla shoved some papers beneath his nose. "I need you to..."

Nice, sweet, caring Vince, he thought sarcastically. Caitlin needed someone and the superterrific, infallible, all-around-perfect man Vince was going to be it.

Darla sighed, loudly. "Joe, you're not paying attention to me. I think I should be insulted."

"I'm sorry," he muttered, rubbing his face. "I didn't mean to hurt your feelings."

"You didn't." Her voice was kind. Amused, but kind. "But stop mooning over her. It's unattractive."

"I'm not mooning."

"Sure about that?"

"Yeah." Vince would probably offer consolation, maybe a hug, and that would lead to a kiss. Dammit! Joe knew how incredibly Caitlin kissed, so he could only surmise where *that* would lead, and— His heart stopped, ice-cold at the thought. "No!"

Darla smothered a smile and shot him an innocent look. "Is that no, you don't want to expense your equipment out all in one period?" She tucked her tongue in her cheek. "Or no, you don't want Vince to get a piece of my assistant?"

In one smooth, angry motion, he rose and moved to the door. "She's *my* assistant, dammit. You can't have her."

Darla let her smile loose. "Joe, sweetie? Give her a kiss for me, would ya?"

"Bite me," he retorted, and slammed the door.

9

CAITLIN DIDN'T KNOW if she could handle the humiliation, but at this point, she was almost beyond caring.

"Nice," Chastity murmured, sugar dripping from her voice. She held her wrist up to the light, where the tennis bracelet glittered with three carats of white diamonds. "How much did you say, darling?"

Caitlin glanced at the bracelet and tried to harden her heart at selling off the only piece of jewelry she'd ever gotten from her father. "It's part of the set," she managed to say. "You have the list."

"Yes." Chastity gave her a cool glance, then reappraised the other items spread out over Caitlin's dining-room table. "You're still giving me all the furniture at the price we agreed on?"

It was far, far, less than what everything was worth, Caitlin knew. But despite the fact she'd just gotten a call from the mortgage company, and now knew Joe had bought her some time, she still couldn't afford the place, which only made her all the more desperate. Chastity, snob that she was, was prepared to give her a check today because she ran the private charity auction house that would come to cart Caitlin's stuff away. That the two women used to run in the same circle only added to Caitlin's humiliation.

But what could she do? She needed fifteen hundred to cover the check she'd just written for first, last and security deposit on her new apartment. *Shack* would have been a more accurate term, but it would put a roof over her head, and at the low monthly rent, she could just afford it. The proceeds from the sale of the jewelry would help cover the cost of a new—and very used—car.

She'd also finally figured out that she wanted to go back to college and get a degree, in something involving numbers. She could do it at night, work for Darla during the day—soon as she quit working for Joe—and she'd be fine. Just fine.

Right. And pigs could fly.

In spite of everything, though, a little burst of pride zipped through her. She'd be supporting herself, and it felt so good she almost could have hugged Chastity. Almost.

The knock at the door took her by surprise. So did the sight of Vince standing there.

"Hi," she said, panic welling. *Not this.* She could handle having to sell everything. Having to move. But she couldn't take having a friend watch. "Why aren't you at work?"

"I wanted to help pack."

"No! I mean…I'm fine. I told you on the phone. I'm just fine."

Chastity came up behind Caitlin, and eyed Vince with open curiosity. Caitlin moved to try to cover Chastity's view and prayed the woman would keep her mouth shut.

"You sounded...funny at work," he said in a low voice, keeping his eyes on Caitlin's instead of on the tall, model-beautiful woman behind her. She could have kissed him for that alone, but desperation moved in.

"As you can see, I'm really doing okay." She managed a smile that only made him frown harder.

"Are you sure?"

"Yes, I'm sorry, I don't mean to be rude, but I'm really busy. I'll see you—" She started to close the door, but he blocked her.

"I want to come help you move tomorrow," he said firmly, lifting his gaze for the first time and eyeing Chastity with mistrust.

"Hello, there," Chastity purred, and Vince nodded before looking at Caitlin again.

"I'll come early, okay?"

"Fine." She pressed on the door, knowing it would be faster to agree than argue. His help would be welcome, and so would his support.

"Wait." Vince pulled an envelope from his back pocket. "I brought your paycheck. I thought you could use it."

She took it without much enthusiasm, knowing it wouldn't make a dent. "Thank you. See you tomorrow, Vince." Before he could protest, she shut the door on his tense, worried face.

And felt like a jerk.

"Was that your boyfriend?" Chastity asked slyly. "He's awfully cute for a redhead. All that warm concern and those burning green eyes."

"He's not in your tax bracket," Caitlin said dully, and Chastity laughed.

Caitlin opened her check and did a double take. Joe had given her a raise. A big one. Her heart squeezed painfully. More pity? she wondered. Or something deeper?

"Is Vince part of CompuSoft?"

Lifting her gaze from the surprising amount of money in her hand, she asked, "What do you know about CompuSoft?"

"There's lots of buzz about the company's future." Chastity's eyebrows rose. "And of course, its owner, Joe Brownley."

Caitlin went still, her raise momentarily forgotten. "You know him?"

"I met him once. At one of your father's fantastic parties. I think you were in Paris at the time. Or maybe it was Milan. I can't remember. He's really something."

"My father?"

"Keep up, darling." Chastity again admired the bracelet on her sleek, tanned wrist. "Joe Brownley. He had every woman at that party drooling. And to think, now you work for him."

"Drooling?"

Chastity shook her head. "You sound like a parrot." She sank to the leather couch and ran her fingers lovingly along the back. "I just might keep this one for myself—you have such good taste." She sighed in pleasure and leaned back. "What was I saying? Ah, yes. Joe. A tough-talking, amazing-looking bad boy if I ever saw one. I love them like that, all nasty attitude and an insatiable sexual appetite."

Joe and Chastity. Weak, Caitlin made herself ask, "Did you two…"

"No, I'm sorry to say. But it wasn't for lack of trying on my part, let me tell you. The way that man fills out a pair of jeans could make a grown woman beg for mercy."

"Could we just get on with this?" It hurt. Not losing her things—they'd never really been hers to begin with. Not having to move; since she'd truly begun to crave her own place filled with her own stuff, purchased with her own money.

What hurt was something else entirely, something horrifying.

She missed Joe. Missed his smart-ass comments, his from-the-gut laugh that always jump-started her own. Missed his sardonic grin and his piercing light blue eyes. His deep understanding of life and its intricacies. One day without him, and she ached.

She was in trouble.

"I'll take everything," Chastity said, brandishing her checkbook. "All of it."

The doorbell spoiled the relief. "Who now?" Caitlin muttered as Chastity excused herself for a minute, needing to use the telephone.

Caitlin made her way past the open boxes

she'd already started to pack. At the front door, she hesitated, putting a hand on her inexplicably rapidly beating heart. Then she pulled on the knob, only to have her heart stop completely.

Joe had his arms braced against opposite sides of the jamb. His head had dropped between his shoulders, so that when she opened the door, she could have leaned forward an inch and kissed him.

He lifted his face and pierced her heart with his gaze. He didn't move, didn't smile, just looked at her.

Her entire body responded, going weak and strong at the same time. Every sense became heightened so that she felt his look as she would a touch. When she spoke, her voice wavered. "You paid the mortgage on this place until the end of the month. Then you gave me a raise."

"Ask me in, Caitlin."

That would be a disaster. She lifted her paycheck and waved it under his nose. "Why, Joe?"

"Ask me in and I'll tell you."

"Was it guilt? Or pity?"

"All right," he said evenly, pushing past her to step into the foyer. "I won't wait to be asked."

"Joe—"

"Where's Vince?"

She narrowed her eyes at his low, deceptively soft voice. "How did you know he was here?"

"Where is he?" His jaw tightened as he tried to peer around her. "Upstairs?"

"Up— Of course not!" She put her hands on her hips. "I don't want you here. I—"

He gripped her waist and hauled her to him. She felt as though she'd stepped off a cliff into thin air, as if she were falling in slow motion, slipping, gliding in weightlessness. Her heart beat hard and high in her chest. "Back off." She grabbed handfuls of his hair, meaning to push him away, but somehow ending up pulling him closer instead.

She shook. So did he, she could feel his muscles ripple against her. Their eyes locked, her breath came even quicker. "Joe—"

He claimed her mouth with his. She opened to him, hot and hungry. Hands still clasped in his hair, she changed the angle of the kiss and dived deeper, swallowing his incoherent masculine murmur of pleasure.

She wanted him, not just to hold, not just for a few stolen kisses and not just for comfort, though she wanted that, as well. She wanted him in a way that she'd never wanted anyone before. *Crazy*, she told herself. *Insane*. She couldn't afford to be thinking about this, about him. Not with her world falling apart. But she kept kissing him. Kept holding him.

He lifted his mouth from hers, but kept her close. "If you let Vince do that…"

Slowly, the words computed past her own dazed brain. "You came here because you thought I could…with Vince…that we…" With a sound of pure frustration, she pushed him away. "How could you even think it?"

Bitterly disappointed, she tried to move past him.

Joe caught her around the waist and placed her between the wall and his muscled body. There was no doubt that he was angry when he kissed her this time, but he kept at it, nibbling and possessing until the temper evaporated into hot, delicious passion and she was kissing him back with everything she had.

When he finally released her, her body throbbed and tingled. It only marginally satisfied her to see his chest heave with his own unsteady breathing.

With a surprisingly gentle touch, he tucked her wayward hair behind her ear. "I'm sorry. You confuse me."

"It makes two of us," she assured him. "I didn't even let Vince in, Joe. And he didn't *force* his way in, either."

"I never claimed to be a gentleman, princess."

She stared at him, painfully aware of her body's response to his presence. She vibrated with it. "I still can't believe what you thought, or how much I care what you thought." She slapped her paycheck to his chest. "Keep your pity."

"Pity had nothing to do with it. You earned it. Why didn't you tell me you could do more than answer phones?"

"I *did* tell you!"

Chastity came into the room, and oblivious to the thick tension, she announced, "Here's a check, darling. I'm paying for everything. *Everything.* So don't even think about cheating me when the men come tomorrow with the truck—*Oh.*" At the sight of Joe, she dropped her businesslike tone and switched to sex kitten in the blink of an eye. "Isn't this interesting?"

Caitlin dropped her head back on her shoulders and stared heavenward. *Haven't I learned enough humility?*

"So nice to meet you again," Chastity said sweetly, holding out her hand to Joe. "I hear so much about you these days."

"You can't believe any of it," Joe assured her. "Unless it's all good."

Caitlin rolled her eyes. Chastity practically preened. "Very little of what's said about you is good, Joe. Mostly...*outrageous.*"

"Outrageous, huh? Haven't lost my touch, then." His eyes sharpened slightly. "What brings you here, Chastity?"

"Oh, we go way back," Caitlin said quickly. "Don't we, Chastity?"

"Old friends?" Joe smiled and nodded, as though he understood perfectly. What he really understood was that Caitlin seemed desperate to break up this conversation. "That's nice. Funny how Caitlin would pick today to socialize, seeing how she's moving tomorrow."

"And since I'm so busy," Caitlin interrupted, trying to pull him to the door, "you'd better get back to work and let me get to it. Thanks for coming—"

"Looks like you have a lot left to do," he said smoothly, evading her hands. "Maybe I should help you pack."

"Didn't Caitlin tell you?" Chastity laughed, managing to make the sound bubbly and full of pity at the same time. "I'm saving her pretty little hide, so to speak. I'm taking most of her things—on generous donation, of course—and using them for a charity auction next week."

Joe looked at Caitlin. She stared at something fascinating on the floor. She seemed pale, dispirited, and Joe felt sick.

Chastity glanced at her narrow gold Rolex. "Oops, gotta run! I'll be back in the morning with a truck and a couple of hunks to load everything." She scribbled something down on a scrap piece of paper, and as she walked past Joe, she stuffed it into the front pocket of his jeans, damn near fondling him in the process. He took it out and wasn't surprised to see her phone number and address. "Wait a minute."

"No," Caitlin leaped to action and rushed up behind Chastity to open the door for her. "She can't wait—she's in a hurry. So are you. Scoot now, Chastity, I'll see you."

He could fix this, Joe thought with a surge of unfamiliar panic. Otherwise, she'd lose everything, and he knew how it felt to own nothing. "Caitlin—"

"Leave it alone," she whispered frantically

behind Chastity's back. *"Please,"* she added so bleakly, he swallowed his protests and let her show Chastity out.

When the woman was gone, Caitlin turned to him, her face tight and drawn. "I want you to go now."

How long had it been since he'd felt so helpless? It had been a mistake to kiss her, to touch her again. She made him feel things he shouldn't. Made him want things he didn't want to want. There'd been plenty of times in his life he could have had a shot at a future with someone and he'd chosen not to. It was too late for him now, far too late. He wanted to be alone.

And maybe if he kept repeating it to himself, he'd believe it. He'd believe he didn't want this woman in his life, *really* in his life. "Caitlin."

She held up a hand. "I need to be alone," she said quietly, dignity humming. "I *want* to be alone."

"I can't leave you. Not like this." He moved close, but at the last minute, stopped short. What right did he have to hold her? To offer comfort? He wasn't a long-term bet, and she deserved no less. Clasping his hands behind his back to keep them off her, he drew a deep breath. "Have you eaten?"

She gaped at him. Then laughed. "That sounded suspiciously like a question from a man who cared. But that couldn't be, because you would never let yourself do something as foolish as that, would you, Joe?"

"I'm trying to help you." He refused to rise to the bait, though his temper stirred. "I'm trying to offer support."

"Why?"

"Because we're friends."

"No." Sadly, she shook her head. "Friends trust one another, Joe. And you have a real problem with that. You can't let go enough to trust me."

"I care about you," he stated gruffly. "And I'm tired of you throwing it back in my face."

She looked at him, startled. "I'm sorry for that," she said softly. "I know it's not easy for you to care, and I have no right to make you feel as if it's not welcome. It is." She took the few remaining steps between them. Gently, she touched his chest, resting one hand lightly over his steadily beating heart. Watching her fingers, she whispered, "I care about you also, Joe. Far too much."

Beneath her hand, his heart beat faster. "I don't want you to," he said so low she nearly missed it.

For a moment, she stood there, head bowed. Then she raised a wet gaze to his. "I know. But that's just the way it is." Reaching behind him, she opened the front door, inviting him to leave her alone.

10

HE WAS TOUCHING HER, finally touching her. He ran his fingers down the length of her body, making her shiver with delight, anticipation. When he kissed her, slow, deep, lazy kisses that made her weak with pleasure and dizzy with desire, she moaned and begged him for more.

He pushed the blanket down, away from her, and the moonlight glowed over their bodies. His was perfect, hard and rippled and pulsing with life. She'd always felt hers was too soft, too...much, but he whispered how beautiful she was, how good she tasted, and at the needy heat in his eyes, she believed him.

For the first time in her life, she felt truly beautiful. Desirable.

As he kissed her again, he touched her—her face, her throat, her back, her legs, then back up again, stopping at the part of her burning for him.

As he lifted his head, Joseph's light eyes held hers. "I want you," he whispered thickly. "So much." His fingers skimmed over her, lightly, teasing, until she arched up against his hand.

"I want you, too." She clasped her hands around him, holding him close. "I love you, Joe. So much."

He stilled. "No," his low, shaky voice came. "You don't know me."

"*I know enough.*"

His eyes burned brightly. "*I'm...not an easy man.*" His voice was strangled with emotion. "*And God knows I don't deserve you, but Caitlin, don't leave me. Don't ever give up on me.*"

She started to shake her head, but his fingers worked their magic, and her entire body started to shake. "*Joe!*" she called out, on the very edge and teetering crazily....

SHE WOKE UP, twisted in her sheets, damp with perspiration and breathing as if she'd just run a marathon.

A dream. Just a dream. The most real, most perfect dream she'd ever had.

She was alone in her moonlit bed, which was scattered with moving boxes. On an empty shelf sat a porcelain kitty, filled with rose petals. It had been her first purchase for this place, and she hadn't wanted to pack it because then it would be real.

She was leaving.

She lay in her bed, *by herself*, breathless, shaking, alone. Alone and...hot. Very hot.

She had fallen in love with Joe.

She hadn't meant to, but it had happened and now she was really in trouble because he'd never allow himself to love her back. She could give and give until she was exhausted, and still, Joe would never give it back.

Trembling in unfulfilled passion, Caitlin did

the only thing she could. She dropped her face to her pillow and burst into tears.

SATURDAY MORNING DAWNED bright and early. Too early, Caitlin thought with a moan and flipped over, burrowing under the covers.

Her body still tingled, still felt a little neglected, a little needy. That dream had really shaken her, and if she'd had the energy, she might have drowned her sorrows in an ice-cold shower.

When the knock came at the door, she jerked upright with panic as she remembered. It was her moving day. A day of fresh beginnings.

Yeah, right. More like the day she stepped down in the world, from beachfront condo to seedy apartment. Well, it could be worse. She could be pushing a shopping cart and muttering to herself at Venice Beach.

She had to remain positive. She was on her own, supporting herself, a first for her. Unmistakable pride boosted her spirits, as did a healthy amount of fear. Life in the real world, complete with real worries and doubts and insecurities about survival.

A day of change.

The knock came again, not so patiently this time, and with a little laugh, Caitlin leaped out of bed. Vince had kept his promise to come help, to bring the twins and Amy. The thought of having friends around cheered her considerably.

And if a little part of her wished it were Joe,

she shoved that thought from her mind as she pulled on a denim miniskirt and a tank top. Joe had no place in her life.

No place at all, she thought as she wrenched open the front door a minute later and faced...the man of her dreams.

He wore his black jeans with a black polo shirt that was actually tucked in today. His scowl matched the clothing, forcibly reminding her of that modern-day pirate again. And now that she knew he even *kissed* like a renegade, her knees went a little weak at the sight of him. He seemed so big, so tall. She wished she'd put on her platform sandals for some desperately needed height and confidence.

"Joe." Was that her voice, all breathless and excited? She cleared her throat and tried again. "What are you doing here?"

Joe wished to hell he knew. What he *did* know was that he'd never felt so lonely as he had last night. For the first time in his life, he'd felt a deep, burning need to be with someone who cared about him.

To allay that need, he'd looked elsewhere, but had found no one. There'd only been one other person he'd let into his life, but Edmund was gone now. In an attempt to bring the man back fresh into his head, Joe had finally gone through his thick copy of the will. What he'd discovered at the back of the file had stunned him—a personal note from the dead. From Edmund, the note was in his pocket right now.

Joe,

If you're reading this, it's over for me. To be honest, it's been over for a while now. I invested too heavily these past years, and the price is high. All my assets will go to my investors—except CompuSoft, which was always yours in heart anyway.

Make sure you give Caitlin that job we talked about. It'll be all she has—there's nothing left to give her. She will have to learn to take care of herself now, and there's nobody in the world who can do that better than you.

Teach her, Joe. I know you'll resent this intrusion, but I also know you'll help show her what I couldn't. Please, for my sake, don't tell her how stupid I've been. Let me have that at least, but help her.

She'll need you.

Best always, Edmund.

Sick to the depths of his soul, Joe had lain awake all night. Edmund had faced financial disaster, and he hadn't known. Caitlin had been suffering because of it, and he hadn't paid attention. She'd even proved herself over and over, and he had closed his eyes to it.

All those times he'd been so rough. So cruel. She'd given everything she had in the first adverse situation of her life, fighting like a trooper to survive, and he'd done little but groan about the trouble she'd been. Edmund would have been ashamed of him, and Joe had never felt so disgusted in all his life.

"Joe?" Caitlin was looking at him expectantly. "Why are you here?"

"You're letting that Chastity woman take everything, every possession you have, rather than accept my help," he said in a very controlled, very soft voice. "I hate that, Caitlin."

"Do you?"

Gently, he pushed his way in, his mood darkening when he saw the scores of boxes lining the place.

"Why didn't you didn't let me help you?"

"Maybe I wanted to do it myself."

He looked so startled at that, Caitlin had to laugh. "What's the matter? Didn't think the spoiled brat would be able to do it?"

"No," he said with brutal honesty, meeting her steady gaze. "I didn't. But that was before I knew you. I'm beginning to realize you're capable of just about anything."

"I am." Unable to stand there looking at him and not remember her dream, that delicious, perfect dream where he'd touched her with those big, warm hands and sent her to heaven, she turned away.

"Is that what you're wearing to move in?"

She glanced down at herself. Her ribbed, shocking-pink tank top was appliquéd with a huge happy face on the chest. She felt comfortable. Definitely fashionable. But just not quite tall enough... "Yes, it is, but just a sec," she exclaimed, and ran up the stairs.

"Sorry, Chastity," she murmured, and reached into one of the ten huge boxes of shoes she'd agreed to sell. "You'll have to do without these."

After she had the clear, high plastic platform sandals on, she felt better. Much better. She left her room, grabbing the porcelain kitty filled with rose petals, deciding on the spot she wasn't giving that up, either.

At the top of the stairs, she smiled down to an impatiently waiting Joe. She thought she was hot stuff now. Really, really untouchable.

As she reached the second stair, the heel of her right shoe caught. Without warning, she bounced down the stairs on her butt. Rose petals rained down as they spilled out of her porcelain kitty.

When she hit bottom, Joe was right there, on his knees, face grim. "You okay?" Rose petals shimmered in his hair, on his shoulders. "Caitlin! Answer me, dammit."

The only thing hurting at the moment was her pride. Well, and maybe the rug burn she'd just gotten on her tender backside. "I'll live."

He looked so ridiculous with that fierce expression as rose petals fell off his nose, but she didn't dare laugh. She nearly choked holding it in, then she exploded.

He scowled at her laughter. "Are you sure

you're not hurt? I know you couldn't have broken that hard head of yours, but..."

She kept laughing, unable to stop.

His frown faded; he bit his lip. Then he started laughing, too.

"You're unbelievable," he said when he could talk. "Take those damn heels off before you kill me."

"Kill *you*?" she gasped, wiping her tears of mirth.

"Yeah." His voice had gone deep and husky.

She followed his gaze.

Her skirt was hiked up indecently high, exposing a long length of thigh and even a peek at her panties.

She shoved the skirt down, face suddenly hot.

Just like his eyes. "They match," he said unevenly.

Puzzled, she glanced down at the black-and-yellow happy face sewn on the front of her can't-miss-me pink tank top. She thought nothing could embarrass her more than her pratfall down the stairs, but she'd been wrong. Her brilliant pink panties also had happy faces on them, and remembering her graceless slide down the stairs with her skirt up around her ears, she imagined Joe had gotten quite a view of them.

Revenge was simple enough.

When Vince, Tim and Andy showed up, she put them all to work along with Chastity and the men she'd brought.

"This is perfect," Caitlin said casually several hours later.

Tim, Andy and Joe moved by, each staggering under the weight of a huge box. Joe stopped, breath huffing, muscles straining in all sorts of interesting ways. "What's perfect? That we're doing all the work, or that you're the boss for a change?"

She grinned, her revenge complete. "Both!"

LATER VINCE PULLED her aside. "You really okay?"

"Hey, I've got four studs at my beck and call." She took in his designer sweats, and compared them to the jeans of the other men. She had to laugh. "Well, three studs and one really finely dressed man. I can't think of one reason why I shouldn't be just peachy fine."

"Because you're losing everything," he said gently, running his hand up her arm.

"Thanks for the reminder." Why wasn't his touch causing goose bumps? Making her shiver with desire? He was perfect. Any normal woman would have told her so.

But she wasn't normal.

"Are you sure about this, Caitlin?" Vince asked, clearly concerned. "Are you sure you didn't pick too hastily?"

It took her a minute to realize he was talking about her choice of apartment, not the man she'd fallen for.

"I looked up your new address on the map

last night, and I don't think it's such a great neighborhood."

Caitlin knew it wasn't, but she hadn't had much to work with. And she was doing her darnedest not to obsess or dwell, since she hated to do either. But it was getting increasingly difficult to stay cheery with Vince reminding her of everything she'd been trying not to think about. "Well, at least my car won't get stolen."

"Why?" He looked blank and she sighed.

"Because I already got it repossessed. Remember?"

He frowned, for a moment reminding her of another man. The man who was at this moment grappling with a large box, for her, sweat making his skin glisten, exertion making his arms bulge.

Her darn knees went weak and she wasn't even wearing those platforms; Joe had tossed them with great ceremony into the Dumpster.

"Caitlin?" Vince looked at her. "You could come with me. Take your time and find something better."

"I don't think so," Joe said lightly in a voice of steel as he came back inside.

Tim, clearly sensing the sudden tension, clapped his hands and announced cheerfully, "Well, we've got everything you want to bring, Caitlin. I vote we stop for a pizza on the way to the new apartment."

"A vegetarian one," Andy said. "With anchovies."

Tim groaned loudly. "Pepperoni and sausage."

Vince ignored them and stared at Joe. "Have you seen her new place? If you have, you can't possibly believe she'll be safe there."

"But she'll be safe with you?"

Caitlin quickly stepped in between the two. "Okay," she said with a huge, tremulous smile. "Pizza it is. But I'm sorry, Andy. Anchovies make me puke. You can have them on the side."

"I can't believe you said that," Vince said to Joe.

"Why not? You've been drooling after her for weeks now. Falling all over yourself like a lovesick fool."

Vince shook his head in disgust. "And what is it you've been doing, Joe? Because it sure as hell hasn't been working on our program."

"Oh, knock it off, both of you!" Caitlin tried to appeal to their common sense, but the testosterone-fueled men weren't listening. "If you don't, I'm going to get really tough and make you kiss and make up."

In tune to Andy's and Tim's snickers, she pushed each of them out the door toward Vince's van, where everything was loaded. Fast as she could, she told three quick dirty jokes in a row, leaving Tim and Andy in stitches. Even Vince cracked a smile as he hopped into the driver's seat.

But Joe stayed solemn and quiet.

Until they got to her new apartment—which

they discovered had been given away only two hours before. Caitlin's deposit check had bounced.

CAITLIN HAD BEEN TRYING—really she had. But she'd lost every ounce of cheer when over an hour later, she dragged herself back into her condo.

"I'm so sorry," Andy said quietly, taking her hand.

"It's not your fault he didn't have another apartment available," she said wearily. "Don't worry, guys. I'll come up with something."

Joe nodded at the twins, and they reluctantly left.

Vince hovered stubbornly at the door. "I want you to come with me. You're practically homeless."

"No, I'm not. Thanks to Joe here, I can live in this empty place until the end of the month if I want to."

Vince and Joe stared at each other.

"Not that again." She rubbed her head, perilously close to tears. "I can't handle it right now, guys. I'd like to be alone."

Joe's heart cracked at the utterly forlorn expression on her face. He couldn't stand it. "Come with me."

Caitlin's eyes widened. So did his own as he realized what he'd just said, but he wouldn't take it back, not with Vince waiting, watching. Wanting.

"You can come to my place if you'd rather," Vince said quietly.

"Vince—"

"You can stay with me as long as you like."

Immeasurable sorrow filled her eyes as she turned to Joseph's head tech. "I'm sorry, Vince. I just…can't."

Vince's confused gaze searched hers a long moment.

"Don't hate me," Caitlin whispered, squeezing his hand. "I know it sounds stupid and cliché, but I really, really need your friendship."

"I'll always be your friend, Caitlin. Always. But I'll probably also always be hoping you change your mind." With a curt jerk of his head toward Joe, he asked, "Do you have any idea what you're getting into?"

"Only vaguely," she admitted.

"Could you stop talking about me as if I wasn't standing right here?" Joe demanded.

"See? He's bad-tempered. Attitude ridden. Mean as hell," Vince said ruthlessly.

"He's also fiercely loyal, generous to a fault, compassionate and the most wonderful man I've ever met, and you know it because he's your best friend."

Vince nodded slowly. "Yes, he is, and I care about him almost as much as I've come to care about you. My condolences, Caitlin."

Caitlin tilted her head, baffled. "For what?"

"You fell in love with him, didn't you?"

Her smile was both dazzling and wobbly. "Yes," she whispered.

And Joseph's heart stopped.

11

VINCE'S SMILE was bittersweet. "I'm glad for him, even if I am jealous as hell." He met Joseph's stunned gaze and shook his head. "Unbelievable, Joe. Your luck keeps holding."

Joe didn't know whether he'd call it luck or not, but either way, he still couldn't speak. Not with his body humming in disbelief, his eyes glued to the woman who'd just declared herself.

"You're the most courageous woman I know," Vince told Caitlin. "And I hope you're patient, too, because you certainly haven't taken the easy road."

She loves me, Joe thought, bowled over by the knowledge. This unbearably sweet, chaotic, intelligent woman loved him, and all he'd given her in return was a hard time and grief.

"I'll be okay," Caitlin said softly, looking at Joe.

He wanted to hold her, never let her go. He wanted to run like hell and never look back. She deserved better, far better. He'd never been able to handle intimacy. Never. To think he could now was foolish. Worse, he would hurt her. *He'd* get hurt.

The fear of it overwhelmed him, which was

ironic. He wasn't afraid of much. Just a lush, beautiful blonde whose smile and innate kindness knocked him for a loop.

Vince leaned close and gave Caitlin a hug. Joe told himself he wouldn't hurt his best friend unless he kissed her, but then Vince did exactly that, on the cheek.

Caitlin kissed him back, sniffed and opened the door for him. "See you Monday, Vince. Thanks. For everything."

Vince smiled once and was gone.

Joe didn't know whether he was relieved or terrified. Both, he decided a minute later when Caitlin turned around and walked into her empty living room. "Chastity's clearly finished," she said. "Everything's gone."

Maybe she could ignore what had just happened, but he couldn't. "Why did you pick me, Caitlin?"

"I wonder if she took the toaster?" She sighed deeply. "I wanted her to because it was an antique, but whoever buys it won't know you have to turn the bread halfway through or you get burned toast."

"Caitlin."

She was wringing her fingers, and her voice came low and fast. "Well, I'd hate to have someone pay good money for the thing and feel like they got ripped off—"

"Caitlin." He moved up close to her, knowing she was as nervous as he was.

"And the cord! Oh, God. I forgot to tell her it

occasionally catches fire, and you've seen my luck with such things. Do you think I should call her? Because—"

"The damn toaster is gone." He grabbed her shoulders, whipped her around. "Now talk to me."

"I know the toaster's gone!" she shouted unexpectedly. "*Everything* is gone. Do you think I can't see that?" She threw off his touch. "I have eyes in my head, you know!" Her voice cracked. "I'm not a…complete idiot."

Then, to his utter horror, she burst into tears.

"Ah, hell," he said to the empty room, and pulled her into his arms. "I'm sorry," he said gruffly. "I'm so sorry."

"You're only sorry you're the one that's left to deal with me." Her tears soaked his shirt and destroyed his heart.

Selfish, he called himself silently, as quiet sobs shook her body. Holding her close, he ran his hands gently over her back and shoulders. Selfish to enjoy holding her so much, when she was hurting so badly.

"I'm tired of being alone," she said on a sniff.

Tell her, his conscience urged. *Tell her that her father didn't abandon her on purpose, that he had no choice. Tell her you're the jerk for not reading the letter sooner.* But he'd been asked to remain silent by the only man who ever showed him kindness and he couldn't break that promise.

Caitlin squeezed him, hiccuping, and she felt

so small, so defenseless...so perfectly right in his arms.

"You smell like roses," she said finally, sliding her hands up around his neck.

It felt so good to have her touch him, he shuddered at the contact. "I should. I took a bath in them, remember?"

"I'm sorry."

"Those shoes were ridiculous."

"Hey, I needed my height. Extra boost of confidence, you know."

His smile faded as he stroked her hair and rubbed his cheek against the top of her head. He hated that she continually felt self-conscious about herself, knowing that a good portion of that just might be his fault. "Did I ever tell you I'm rather fond of petite women that I can tuck in close and wrap myself around?" He tightened his arms to prove his point.

"No." Her voice was breathless. "You've told me very little about yourself." Warily, she lifted her head. "Are you really?"

"Really." Of its own accord, one hand skimmed down her spine, cupped her bottom and very purposely rubbed her against the painfully hard part of him that could prove his point.

Her mouth opened, as if she couldn't get enough air.

"And here's the really ironic part," he told her in a stage whisper. "Curvaceous blondes are my wildest fantasy."

She lifted her head. Her curtain of gold hair

tickled his chin. Those beautiful, drenched eyes of hers met his. And heaven help him, but he recognized some of the emotion there. Need. Hunger. Desire. His body reacted with matching emotions, fast and hot, leaving him shaken, for he'd never felt that way about anyone. "Caitlin...come with me?"

"Where to?"

"My place." He took her hand.

She resisted. "That's not a good idea."

"Probably not," he agreed. "But I'm not leaving you here alone." He hesitated, cupped her cheek and met her uncertain gaze. "Let's stop fighting this and follow through with it for once, okay?"

She bit her lip and studied him for a long moment, searching for he could only imagine what. Apparently, she found it.

"Okay," she whispered.

SHE FELL ASLEEP in his car on the way to his house. When she felt herself being lifted into a pair of strong arms, hoisted up against a hard, warm chest, she bit back her drowsy grin.

"Oh, Vince. I had no idea you felt so good."

Joseph's arms tightened around her and he growled, making her laugh. Her arms snaked around his neck, and she buried her face into his throat.

"Say my name," he demanded.

"Joe," she whispered obediently, winning

herself a quick, hard hug. "Mmm. You smell good," she murmured, inhaling deeply.

"You're awake," he accused. "Why am I carrying you into my house?"

It was a lovely house. Small, inexplicably cozy.

And messy.

She had a quick view of high vaulted ceilings, airy rooms, magazines and books scattered haphazardly throughout...his home.

Uncertain yet tingling with anticipation, she closed her eyes again.

She had the weightless sensation of going up stairs. She held him tight and kept her eyes closed. "Did I ever tell you I fantasize about this modern-day pirate?" She felt him pause, could feel the weight of his curious stare. It almost made her giggle. "He's tall, dark and so gorgeous and he takes me into his cabin and bounces me onto the—" The sentence ended on a scream as he tossed her into the air.

She hit a soft, giving bed and bounced high. Her eyes flew open. They were in a large bedroom, with dark oak furniture. There were clothes and more books scattered around, not that the mess surprised her; she'd seen his office.

What *did* surprise her was that she was sprawled on the biggest bed she'd ever seen. With forest-green, soft, Joe-scented bedding that she wanted to bury her nose in.

He laughed roughly and followed her down

on the bed. "Do I ravish you now, fair maiden? Or after I tie up your crew?"

"Now, please." The words popped out of her mouth before she could stop them. He lowered himself to her, bracketing her body with his arms.

And it was then that trickle of doubt spurted. Just a trickle, though, because he was tall and dark and oh so gorgeous. "Joe, wait a sec—"

"Pirates wait for no one," he growled in a voice that sent delicious shivers running over her skin.

His tough, lean body pressed against hers, holding her pinned where she'd dreamed about being. But that was her dream, not his. "Joe...this isn't just because you feel sorry for me, is it?"

He blinked, then knelt in the bed, pulling her up with him so that they were face-to-face. "What?"

"We both know I'm not exactly your type."

He stroked her cheek. "I told you I fantasize about you. I meant it."

"You had to say that."

She made a move to leave the bed, and he stopped her, putting his hands on her hips. "What is this? I want you. You have to know that."

"You don't just feel bad because I cried?"

"You're kidding me, right?" Taking her hand, he pressed it down between their bodies, holding it up against the fly of his jeans, and his erection. "If anyone should feel bad for anyone," he announced, his eyes crossing with lust when she caressed him through the fabric, "then feel sorry for me. For *this*." Unable to help himself, he thrust into her hand, groaning when she squeezed gently. "I've been in this pathetic state since the day you walked into my office weeks ago and smiled at me, and it has absolutely nothing to do with pity!"

"Oh," she breathed, her eyes bright and luminous, sensuous and innocent at the same time. Just looking at her had heat spearing his body, weakening his limbs with a needy languor.

She kept on touching him, forbidden delight and discovery lighting her face as her fingers explored him through his jeans. "I did this to you?" she asked in wonder.

"Yeah. *You*," he said, grabbing her waist. "You. Only you, Caitlin."

Her eyes met his, full and warm. "I love you, Joe."

It should have turned him off to hear the words, but instead they had the opposite effect. "I can't give you more than this," he told her, his voice rough and torn as he pushed against her hand mindlessly. "No promises. I can't."

"I know," she whispered, sighing deeply when he flexed his buttocks again. "Don't worry, Joe. This is enough for me."

It wasn't, shouldn't be, and he wanted to tell her so, but then she planted her wet, open mouth on his throat and her fingers moved on him again, and he was lost to reason. Lost to anything but what she was doing to him.

Then she let him go, and he thought he would die right there on the spot. So much emotion swirled in her eyes; heat, need, desire...and then with one fluid motion, she pulled off her ribbed tank top with the happy face. She was wearing nothing beneath but glorious, proud, full curves.

"Caitlin." He said just that, just her name, because he could hardly breathe, but she covered herself with her arms. The most difficult thing he'd ever done was to bite back his own raging needs, to soothe and excite. He wanted to see her wild, out of control. For him. He ran a finger down her arm, watching as goose bumps rose. He touched her hair reverently, then eased it aside to kiss the sensitive spot beneath her ear.

His fingers, light as air, played on her throat, then moved to the back of her neck. Stroking, teasing, always barely touching, but still she covered herself, not wanting to stop, he knew, but not knowing how to make him continue.

With his large, warm, tender hands, he cupped her face and tilted it up. "You're so beautiful," he whispered. "So very beautiful, Caitlin." Then he kissed her, stealing any breath she had left. That warm, sexy mouth deepened the connection, his powerful body pressing into hers. When he finally raised his head, she moaned in protest.

"Be sure, Caitlin," he said softly. "I won't have you regretting this."

"I have nothing to regret," she promised. The words were no sooner out of her mouth than his head descended. Each kiss got hotter, wetter, deeper. He ran his hands down her arms to her elbows.

"Why would you try to hide such an incredible body?" he wondered hoarsely.

"Because I'm embarrassed." She closed her eyes. "I'm too…"

"Too perfect." He finished her sentence in a husky whisper. "Don't tell me you're hiding something. Tan lines? Freckles?"

"Both," she admitted with a choked laugh, which died on a harsh intake of breath when his fingers explored the soft flesh spilling out above and below her crossed arms. "Oh…*oh*. Joe, hurry."

"Don't rush me," he murmured. "I want to see and touch and taste each little bit as we go."

She had melted at his tender touch, but his words finished the job.

Gently, Joe took her hands and pulled them away from her body. His gaze held hers, and she'd never felt so exposed or so aroused in her entire life.

"No, don't do that. Don't be embarrassed," he told her. "Save it for when you sail down the stairs on your ass. Or when you blow up my coffeemaker. But not here. There's no room for it. Only for you, and me and what we make each other feel." Without another word, he lowered his head, splaying his hands on her bare back to draw her close, and opened his mouth on her breast.

Fire speared through her, and Caitlin bit her lip to keep any sounds she might make inside, but it was difficult, made more so by what he continued to do to her. With his tongue, he teased, using a maddening light touch, then suckled hard and strong.

She was burning up. Her toes were curling. Her insides were churning, shaking. So were her legs. She shook her head to clear it. Still, her body raced, each pulse a desperate, needy beat. "I feel...funny," she whispered, realizing she was holding tight to his shirt with a death grip.

"I feel overdressed." Straightening, he whipped his shirt off, and the light that had been too stark only a moment before became a blessing. Rugged, lean and rangy, he was quite simply the most magnificently made man she'd ever seen. His gaze held hers as his fingers went to the button on his jeans. It opened and...

Oh, how could she have forgotten? "Joe—" She let out a disparaging sound. "I don't know quite how to tell you this," she moaned.

His fingers stilled. "You could start by opening your eyes," he suggested quietly.

She did, then wished she hadn't. His body was incredible. His chest drew her fingers. She couldn't help herself, the tensed muscles, the light, springy hair that tapered down and disappeared into his open jeans...

Capturing her wandering hands in his, he looked at her. "Tell me now, before this goes any further. A change of heart?"

"Not exactly." Bravely, she met his hot, frustrated gaze. "I'm sort of a...virgin."

12

"SORT OF?" Joe let out a choked laugh. "You're *sort of* a virgin? How is that?"

"Because I haven't done it before."

"Caitlin." His rough voice held a hint of a smile. "*How* is it you've never done this before?"

Self-conscious now, she turned from him and once again crossed her arms over herself. "I know you probably thought I had lots of experience. I let people think that because…"

"Because?"

This wasn't the time to shrink back and try to save her feelings, or her pride. "Because then they know I mean it when I say back off."

"Ah…the curse of being desirable."

"I don't understand it." She wished she had her shirt back, but in her haste to jump him, she'd tossed it dramatically across the room. "But nobody looks beneath the surface."

"Or past the checkbook," he said in her ear, making her jump.

"I guess you do understand."

"What I don't understand is why you were going to let me have you." With terrifying tenderness, he pulled her back against his chest, crossing his arms over hers to hold her close.

It took every ounce of courage she had, but at this point, there was nothing to lose. Turning in those warm, capable arms, she met his questioning, and yes, still passionate, gaze. "Because I love you, Joe. I wanted you to be my first."

His eyes were bright, eloquent. "I thought we weren't going to make promises."

"I don't expect one back," she assured him, pulling his head down to hers. "Please, Joe. Love me. Just for now."

Her lips clung to his, warm and wet. Sensuous and innocent. *Just for now,* Joe promised himself. His eyes never left hers as he stepped out of the rest of his clothes. "Don't regret this. I won't be able to stand it if you do."

"I won't." Her gaze was glued on him, her eyes wide and huge as she unabashedly stared at his proud, heavy sex. "You're so beautiful, Joe. All virile and...hard."

On a laughing moan, he lay down, wrapped her in his arms and held her to him while his mouth ravaged hers again. "*Hard* being the key word here." He slipped his hands beneath her skirt, caressing her thighs, playing with the tiny panties he knew were covered with happy faces. "I've wanted to take these off since the moment I got a front-row view of them on the landing."

She closed her eyes, her face flushing. Laughing, Joe kissed her until she was flushed with passion, not embarrassment. He loved the texture of her—all soft and dewy, he discovered as he removed the last of her clothing. Loved, too, the way her body quivered at his every touch. Lowering his head, he nuzzled at her, kissing and nipping until she was squirming and burning and restless beneath him.

Lifting his head, he whispered, "Every time I was a jerk at work, it's because I wanted to do this." His thumbs made passing caresses over the tips of her tight, aching breasts, and he watched her body's response, the way she panted for air, how her nipples puckered and beaded. When he drew her into his mouth again, she arched off the bed and into his arms.

His hands ran down over her stomach, her thighs and back up between her legs. She caught her breath when he touched her there, then again when his touch deepened. Tossing her head back, she fisted her hands in the sheets and pushed up against his fingers, whimpering shamelessly.

"Good?" he asked.

"More."

She was the sweetest, most desirable woman he'd ever seen, and for the moment, she was his. "Yes," he promised. Her slippery heat coated his fingers and he moaned. "Yes, more."

Her body tightened as he stroked her slowly, every muscle clenched. His fingers continued their sensuous play, giving her what she'd wanted, and she whispered his name, her voice torn between need and panic.

"It's all right." He drowned in the pleasure of

watching her discover desire. "I'm right here to catch you."

She was on a tightwire, grappling and struggling for balance. She hadn't expected this. Had thought it would be fast. Reckless. Even painful. What she got was hot, delicious sensation. "Joe!" She wriggled, but the heat just consumed her all the more. "Where's my *more*?"

"For someone new at this, you're awfully bossy." He kneeled between her legs. "I like that in a woman." He put on a condom before she could stop him. It wasn't that she didn't want to be protected, but she wanted to participate in everything. Before she could complain, he was kissing her again and she could participate in that, oh yes, she could.

Joe tasted her lips, her jaw, the precise spot on her throat where the pulse frantically leaped, then took her mouth again, shaken with the force of his own need. And those fierce little sounds that escaped the back of her throat were the most arousing he'd ever heard. He heard her sigh, then when he nudged at her hot, wet center, she gasped.

"Okay?"

"Yes," she murmured, opening for him. "More. You promised."

"Hold on to me, Caitlin. Hold on tight."

Her arms slipped around him. His mouth closed over hers as he slid into her inch by inch. When she cried out, he froze in terror that he'd hurt her, but she shifted her hips, lifting experimentally. "Oh," she breathed, drawing him in deeper, snugger, tighter. "Oh, I like it."

His hands shifted from her hips to brace on either side of her face where, from behind a haze of deep hunger, he watched her for any signs of pain or discomfort. She shot him a dazzling smile, and he saw only pleasure—dazed, dark pleasure.

"There's even more, isn't there?" she asked hopefully, making him both groan and laugh at the same time.

She met him stroke for mind-blowing stroke. And in her eyes, he saw everything he'd feared. Warmth, affection, acceptance, heat, need. Love. He saw her soul, and his mirrored back. He knew that alone should have brought the most fear of all, but miraculously, it didn't.

Beneath him, her eyes went wide, her mouth opened in a surprised O as she began to tremble and quiver. He tried to hold back, to prolong it for her, but his body finally betrayed him as she convulsed. Her shudder worked through him and became his, swirling and demanding, and he buried his face in her neck. She sobbed out his name as she climaxed, and clenching her fisted hands in his, he let himself go with her.

CAITLIN WOKE FIRST, to the sound of a light spring rain. Joe held her as he slept, her back to his front, his arms possessively tight. One of his large hands, fingers spread wide, was low on her belly. The other had tangled itself in her hair.

One of his thighs was pressed between hers, and for a minute, she allowed herself to snuggle in deeper, surrounded by his warmth.

She'd made love, for the first time in her life. Giddiness welled, as did a blissful wonder. She'd never known...never expected it to be so spectacular.

He had made it that way, she thought, joy flooding her. He'd been fierce and wild, and gentle and tender. And afterward, he'd carefully cleaned her with a warm washcloth, expressing concern, but it hadn't been necessary.

She felt fantastic.

And ready for more.

His breathing was deep and even, and she decided to show mercy as she'd obviously exhausted him.

The scent of the rain on the air drew her, as did her curiosity about the house. She'd only caught a short glimpse of it. She slipped out of his arms, then stopped to admire his tough, rangy body, only half-covered by the sheet.

He was...heart stopping. And, for now, hers.

The air was hot, muggy, so she walked nude to his dresser and stopped short, baffled at the reflection. Her hair exploded around her face in loose curls. Her lips were red and swollen, her eyes bright with light.

She looked...like a wild woman in love, one who'd just been shown how much she was loved back.

Did Joseph love her?

She twisted to see the still sleeping form on the bed. He was magnificent, sprawled in all his glory. He certainly lusted after her, and she blushed remembering exactly how much.

But did he love her?

She sighed, suddenly discontent. She stepped out onto the dark patio. His house faced the ocean, giving her an incredible view of heavy waves lit only by whatever weak moonbeams managed to evade the clouds.

A jag of lightning flashed across the sky, and a second later thunder rolled. The roof of the deck was slatted and the cool rain fell through, wetting her. Shivering a little in spite of the hot air, she stood there, face upturned to the mist, loving the erotic feel of the cool drops landing on her hot body.

MY GOD, JOE THOUGHT as he stepped onto the deck. *That's a sight.* Caitlin stood there with her head tipped back, the slim column of her neck exposed, her full breasts thrust out, her legs taut as she rose up on tiptoe, stretching. Her white skin glimmered and shone as the rain ran in small rivulets down her body.

Just standing there watching her take her own pleasure from the rain had him rock hard. He walked up behind her, slid his arms around her slick body. "I thought it was all a dream," he whispered in her ear, taking the soft flesh there between his teeth, drawing goose bumps to her skin.

Arching back, pressing her spine to his chest, she sucked in her breath when his hands spread on her thighs, streaked up her hips, over her belly and captured her wet breasts. "If it was," she moaned, "it's the best dream I ever had." His thumbs flicked over her rigid nipples, making her writhe, her hips rubbing urgently back against his.

"Caitlin." He slid his hand down, down past damp curls and into hot, creamy heaven, thrilling to the soft, dark sounds she made. "Are you sore?"

"No, not yet," she murmured, gripping the railing in front of her for balance and grinding her hips in tune with his hand. "I had no idea...how it would be. I want more, Joe... more."

Whatever she wanted tonight would be hers. Whatever she needed, he'd find a way to give it. The rain fell unnoticed, and the night sang with the sounds of the ocean waves hitting the shore below them.

He kept her from falling as she came, quivering in the pale light, her skin aglow. He held her like that, just held her, with her bottom snugged up to his thighs, with their hearts racing together, and he had to fight against swiftly and greedily taking all that she offered. It wasn't easy, not with her hands urging him as she reached back and gripped his hips, and her body poised and waiting, silently confirming she yearned as much as he. The ache within him became primal and blinding as he absorbed the exquisite feel of her against him.

Nothing would ever be the same again.

Suddenly, there was no reason to rush; there was time. Time for everything. And oh, how he wanted everything, every whisper, every promise, every touch, every single second of this time with her.

Everywhere he touched, she turned something inside him to gold. Despite the misery of his past, she made him feel good, wanted, needed...loved. "You make me feel so alive," he said huskily, kissing his way along her jaw. "So alive."

She twisted her head, and her lips parted for his kiss. The urgency returned tenfold. She pressed back against him, restlessly running her hands up and down his thighs, trying to draw him inside her.

Too fast, he wanted to tell her. He wanted to savor, explore, but he couldn't be gentle or tender now. Nor patient, either, with her fingers digging into him, urging, demanding.

The darkness cocooned them; the rumbling thunder and flash of lightning provided their music. There was no other sound except the frantic roar of their own hearts and harsh, needy breathing. One last time, Joe brought his mouth down to hers, taking her stunned cry into his throat as he gripped her hips and sheathed himself into her from behind, filling her. Not just with his body; even in his confusion, he understood that.

Caitlin threw her head back against his shoulder, her body bowing in slim arch with strain and wonder and abandon. Even as part of his brain struggled to register that he didn't want to love her, didn't want to need her, she was taking him away to a place where there was no reality. Where love didn't hurt. Where he could let himself go.

He closed his eyes and did just that. He'd known, hadn't he, that it would be like this with her. No restraints, no boundaries. No hurt. Nothing and no one but the two of them, soaring as high as the clouds.

"I HAVE NO IDEA why I waited so long to do that," Caitlin said conversationally a short time later. "It was the most fun I've ever had."

"Fun?" He pulled on a pair of sweatpants and laughed shortly. "You nearly sent me to another world, and you thought it was fun?"

He watched her blond head poke out the neck of his shirt as she put it on, and his blood surged again at the way she looked wearing his clothes. "You know what I mean," she said, lifting her gaze and smiling at him.

His throat closed. "Yeah."

"I...uh...you know. Had an orgasm." She blushed gorgeously and he laughed.

"*An* orgasm?" He laughed again. "Princess, you most definitely had more than one."

"Is it always like that?"

His amusement faded. It had *never* been like that. "No, not always."

She was looking at him with such emotion, he nearly lost it right there. His lungs seemed to collapse. He needed her, so damn much. Fear welled, but he beat it back. She wouldn't know, *couldn't* know, unless he told her. And if he didn't tell her, he had nothing to fear. Nothing at all.

But she deserved more than a quick toss in the sheets. She needed a man who would give her a future, a man who could give in to his emotions and love her as she deserved to be loved. She didn't need him further screwing up her life. Hell, she already thought she was in love with him. Delusions, of course. No one could love him, not really. He was trouble. Had an attitude. A temper. He could be a real selfish bastard. He'd once walked away from his family without looking back. He'd taken everything Edmund had given him without questioning Edmund about Caitlin, and what she might need. Caitlin didn't know this, didn't understand, or she could never believe herself in love with him.

He had to walk away now. Had to forget that she could make him laugh, could make life seem more important than work. He had to get over how her chaotic world was as fresh as springwater when compared to his, which was stagnant, dead. He had to forget that her way of living revived his, gave him back the joy of being.

She'd wormed her way into his heart, spreading happiness like wildfire, and he hadn't even noticed it happening. He *had* to forget, or the realization of exactly what it would cost him to walk away would kill him.

She took his hand, and that simply loving, trusting gesture had him swallowing hard.

He'd betrayed Edmund by failing to protect Caitlin. He'd betrayed Caitlin by taking her love and innocence without means to repay it. Any minute, fate was going to come knocking and swipe away any semblance of happiness.

She led him down the stairs. "I'm starving," she said. "I hope you have more food in your house than I do in mine." In the entryway, halfway between his kitchen and the living room, she came to a grinding halt. "I've never seen your place."

He let out a laugh. "Should've opened your eyes when I was playing pirate and hauling you upstairs."

But Caitlin didn't crack a smile. She stared at the beautiful glass-and-stone foyer, looked through the kitchen and then sank to a large window seat in the front room, which overlooked the sea. "You never told me you lived at the beach, too," she said with mock calm while her heart drummed painfully.

"I didn't know where you lived until yesterday."

It was a day for truths, and she had to have

this one. "My father loved the beach. He gave this place to you, didn't he?"

A shadow crossed Joseph's expressive, rugged face. "Yes. Years ago. When I graduated from the college he bullied me into attending."

"I see." Pain slashed through her, and she didn't quite manage to keep it out of her voice. "I'm sorry. I...have to go."

In three strides, he caught up with her at the door. Gently, his heart already dying, he turned her to face him. "I didn't know he didn't pay yours off, Caitlin. I swear to you, until that day we had lunch, I didn't know. Come here. You'll see." He dragged her back through the living room into the kitchen. On the table was a file, which he opened. "The deed for this place," he told her, lifting it up for her inspection.

Attached to it was a quit-claim notice, which even she knew meant Joseph was signing this house over, and out of his name. *To her.*

"I don't understand why Edmund had paid mine off all those years ago, and hadn't done the same for you."

"I do," she said sadly. "It was my own fault. I moved around a lot, was a fickle little thing. He never believed I'd stay in one place for long."

He tossed the document to the table and took her shoulders so he could see into her face. "Whatever his reasons, I can't keep this place while you lose yours. It's wrong, and so was I."

"Wrong? How were you wrong?"

He'd gone a little pale. "I should have done

this a long time ago. I'm ashamed of myself that I didn't. I'm giving you this place."

"No." She backed away from him, holding her hands out to ward him off, because one more touch would have her crumpling, and she had to be strong. "You're not giving it up for me." She walked out of the foyer, and he followed her into the living room. "My father gave it to you," she said, turning around in the large room. "He wanted you to have it."

"I can't keep it." He watched her pace. "You're hurting and I want to make it better."

Caitlin knew there was only one way for Joe to make it better, and that was for him to love her back as hopelessly as she loved him. While she suspected he might feel that way, she was afraid that he was so used to being able to rely on only himself, he'd never be able to tell her. "You can't do this. He loved you, Joe."

"Yes. And I…loved him," he said softly, the words grainy and rusty, as if he'd never said them out loud before. He looked open, and more vulnerable than she thought possible.

He *could* love, she thought with a rush of joy and hope. And knowing that, she knew anything, anything at all, was possible.

"I loved him," he repeated. "God, I did."

Through a haze of tears, Caitlin reached out and hugged him. "I know you did," she said brokenly. "I know."

He clung close and so did she, their bodies warm and snug and comforting. It started out that way at least, but as the seconds ticked on, and as Caitlin thrilled to be needed by him, the embrace turned decidedly sexual. The smooth, sleek skin of his back drew her fingers, and her hips instinctively melded with his.

"Caitlin."

His low voice turned her on, too. Everything about him turned her on. He was unpolished. Physical. Sharply intelligent. Fascinating.

And fiercely aroused.

He looked at her, and it was far more than the heat and hunger that drew her. Whether he knew it or not, he did *need* her, needed her strength and affections. Her love.

She wanted to give it.

She slipped her arms around his neck at the same time that he caught her up against him. His body was strong and hard and grieving. The combination was irresistible.

"Again," she whispered, kissing his jaw, his ear, whatever she could reach. "I want you again."

"No, it'll hurt you," he protested softly. "You'll get sore."

"Don't make me seduce you," she said, and he laughed, turning his face so that their mouths met, only it wasn't the gentle kiss she'd been expecting. Instead, it was deep and wet and long and had them both straining for more.

"Please, Joe," she whispered. "You'll never hurt me."

He moaned, his forehead against hers. "I can't

resist you, not for anything." He dragged her down to the thick carpet, then took her face in his hands and kissed her again, a carnal mating of their tongues, a mimic of what he really wanted to do to her. He touched her first with his hot gaze, then opened the shirt covering her, spreading it wide.

Slowly, he lowered his body to hers, grace and power blending into one. He took her to new heights by just touching her with his magic fingers. He tore off his sweats so they were skin to skin. He was sensual and uninhibited, and he encouraged the same from her, caressing and kissing every inch of her until she was panting his name.

When he slid down between her thighs, replacing his fingers with his lips, she arched up and begged. It wasn't necessary; his open mouth unerringly found her. One stroke from his nimble tongue and she exploded. Instantly. Without control.

Chest heaving, body slick with perspiration, hair sticking to her face, she looked up at the ceiling and blinked in stunned surprise. Her body rippled with aftershocks. "Wow."

"Again," he demanded, cupping her, stroking her back into a frenzy, back to the point of no return, until bright lights blinded her, until her body went taut as a bow, then shuddered again and again.

"Wow," she repeated when she could finally manage as she lay limp and replete on the floor.

Joseph's skin was also slick when he levered himself above her and bridged her body with his arms. "Such a profound statement."

She ran her hands through his hair. "Then how about *more?*"

"Caitlin—"

"Don't make me beg again."

He entered her, then, watching her flushed face carefully. She sighed with pleasure. He pushed deeper. Her breath quickened and so did his, and eyes locked with hers, he pushed deeper still. When he was fully seated within her, they both moaned.

He pressed his forehead against hers. "Tell me you're okay."

"I'm...so much more than okay."

He began to move and she raised her hips to meet his hungry thrusts. Though each one threatened to toss him over the edge, he held back, waiting for her.

When she climaxed, she dug her fingers into his skin and cried out his name, shuddering long and hard. It was more than he could take. Burying his face in her neck, he allowed himself to follow her into oblivion.

"OKAY, YOU CAN SEDUCE ME," he gasped, and she laughed.

They stared at each other, and their smiles faded slowly.

"Please, let me do this for you," he whispered. They were lying entwined on the soft carpeting, looking at the high ceiling, listening to the rain pound the roof. "Please let me give you this place."

"You know, I think I've figured something out." She sat up and slipped his shirt back on with a smile. She loved wearing his clothes. "I don't think my father meant to forget me. He just wanted to show me something."

Guilt stabbed at him, and he wished with all his might Edmund hadn't asked for his silence. She looked so beautiful sitting there covered only by his shirt, still flowing from their love-making.

Beautiful and brave.

But all he could think about was the secret he was keeping from her. The secret his mentor—her father—had asked him to keep.

She was right. Edmund hadn't forgotten her; he'd tried to protect her, the only way he knew. Through Joe.

And Joe had let them both down.

His heart hurt just looking at her. That unwanted panic surged again when he realized what was happening to him. That despite his promises to himself, he just kept falling for her deeper and deeper.

He loved her.

"I think my father just wanted me to learn to support myself, you know?" I always resented him saying that, and because of that resentment, I never bothered to learn when he was alive. But he was right. I can see how selfishly I'd been living. This has helped me grow up, and at twenty-four, it's about time."

He stared at her. "How can you be so generous? So understanding?"

"It's just facts." She reached out and hugged him. His heart broke.

Sorry, Edmund, he pleaded silently. *Forgive me, but I have to do this.*

He had to tell the truth. "Caitlin." His voice was hoarse, and for the life of him he couldn't force himself to return her sweet smile. "I have to show you something."

He drew her to her feet, using the excuse to hold her close one more time, for he held no illusions.

This would be the last time.

"It's upstairs," he said. "Will you come with me?"

"Anywhere," she said simply, and his chest tightened all the more.

In his room, he went to his jeans, which were still lying on the floor. Slipping them on, he pulled out Edmund's letter from the pocket.

Caitlin recognized her father's writing. "What's this?" she asked, looking at him.

"Read it."

"Oh, my God," she breathed, sinking onto the bed as she did just that. "He ran out of money.... He asked you to take care of me." She closed her eyes on the mortification. "And I thought I was doing it on my own." She let out a choked laugh. "Not only did he make you give me a job—he had such a low opinion of me that he thought you would have to help teach me to support myself!"

"No, no Caitlin, it's not like that—"

She leaped off the bed, and though he thought he'd been prepared for her to walk out of his life, he'd been wrong.

He couldn't let her go.

He caught her at the door, barely. "Wait. Caitlin—"

"No." She ripped free, his shirt flying up above her luscious thighs. Her wild hair swung in a curtain when she whipped around to face him. "You knew all along his money was gone. You called me princess, you made fun of me, and you knew!"

"No, no, I didn't. I saw the note for the first time yesterday. I know how this all sounds to you, but you've got to listen." He grabbed her shoulders and jerked her close, as if he could shake the belief right back into her. "Before you came into my life, all I thought about was work. I ate, slept and drank work."

"You still do," she said bitterly, shrugging him off and backing to the door. "What a fool I've been. I thought you were starting to come around, starting to care for me."

"I was. *Am!*"

"Right."

"Caitlin," he said in a grating voice, coming after her, letting pride go because he had no choice. No choice at all. "You have no idea how difficult this is for me to say, but it's the truth. I care for you. More than I ever have for anyone."

"I don't think so. I think this is guilt. It's just you fulfilling a stupid promise you made to my father." Her lovely eyes filled. "And because he meant so much to you, you'll do anything to see the vow through."

"He *did* mean a lot to me. But you've got the promise thing all wrong—"

He was talking to air.

When he caught her on the stairs, she spun on him. "Did you guys get a good laugh at my expense?" Her eyes were stark with pain. "Tim and Andy. And Vince. Was it all a joke? Their help? Their friendship?"

"No. No, Caitlin. God. They worship you. You've got to know that."

"I know nothing anymore," she said sadly, backing from him. "Except that apparently I've been such a burden to you that you couldn't even explain the truth to me."

"You read the letter. He asked me not to tell you. Whether it was pride or love—"

She let out a hard laugh. "Don't fool yourself. He loved *you*, Joe."

She made it to the bottom of the stairs before he caught up with her and hauled her back against him. "It was far more than just a promise," he grated into her ear as she struggled valiantly against him. "And you're not going anywhere. Not even if you did manage to put some pants on."

"Yes, I am."

"You don't have a car."

"I'm a pro at public transportation, believe me."

"Forget it." He entertained some half-baked idea about holding her down on his bed and proving to her in the only way he knew how to show her how much he cared.

"In your mind, you owed him," she panted as she wiggled and shimmied to free herself, grunting when he simply slung her over his shoulder.

"It started out that way, yes. Damn, you're heavy. Ouch—" He snarled through his teeth when she bit him on the shoulder, hard. "But I *did* start to care about you. Hell! I couldn't stop thinking about you." He carried her up the steps, back into his room.

Tossing her to the bed, he watched her eyes darken with anger when she bounced.

"You only thought about me so much because of all the trouble I caused," she accused, furious. Hurt.

When he knelt next to her, she crawled away.

"Don't touch me." She ran around the side of the bed, jerked her skirt off the floor and slid it over her legs. "Don't ever touch me again."

"Dammit, Caitlin."

"No, I mean it," she said when he came after her. "Don't touch me now—I won't be able to resist you if you do." Biting her lip, she looked wildly around, then shoved her bare, petite feet into his large tennis shoes. Her anger faded at the look on his face. "This isn't all your fault," she allowed. "It's mostly mine, actually. I'm an idiot to have fallen for you."

"I fell for you, too," he said quietly.

She straightened and tugged down the hem of his shirt with touching dignity despite the fact that only a fraction of an inch of her skirt stuck out the bottom, and she looked like a little girl playing dress-up. "It came far too late, Joe."

Now he knew real, gut-wrenching fear. The kind he hadn't felt since he'd been a kid with nowhere to go and nothing to eat. "What do you mean?"

"I mean that I have to go."

He reached for her again, but she backed away. Nothing had ever hurt as much as that. "Don't do that," he beseeched her, fighting nasty by going in low and snagging her to him. "Don't back away from me—I can't take it."

"I feel like you betrayed me, Joe. I can't forget that."

"And I can't let you go," he said softly, gentling his hold. With minute care, he cupped her neck and drew her forward so that his mouth could find hers, quietly, slowly, then deeper, until he felt his insides start to crack apart at the emotional pressure built up there. His hands framed her face, then slid down her neck, over her shoulders to mold her body, drawing a soft, needy sound from her.

Then she shoved back, her eyes wide and luminous. "Don't kiss me like that."

"Like what?"

"Like—" Her voice cracked. "Like you love me." Covering her mouth with a shaking hand, she walked away, only to stop, hand hovering over the doorknob when he spoke.

"Don't go, Caitlin."

"I can't stay here with you—it would hurt too much. I want more from you than just...this. I want trust. And love. If I stay, I'll make both of us miserable, and I refuse to do that. I deserve more, Joe, and so do you."

"Wait. Please—" With horror, he realized how close he was to actually begging her. Begging. *God.* He'd been through some unbelievably tough spots before, but he'd never resorted to begging.

She looked at him then, *really* looked at him, and he knew she was seeing past the exterior to the real him. To his deepest of souls. In her eyes, he could see the flicker of life. Of hope. Of love. Hard to accept, when he still hadn't quite let himself believe that she could really love him.

"What should I wait for, Joe?"

The words stuck in his throat.

When he didn't speak, the hope in her eyes went out. Simply extinguished. Liquid brown eyes cold for the first time since he'd met her, she left the room, shutting the door quietly behind her.

All Joe could do was try to swallow past the lump in his throat and watch her go.

He'd ruined everything, and with his eyes wide open.

All because he'd waited too long to trust her with the heart he'd protected from harm for years. All because he'd waited too long to tell her he'd finally, truly, irrevocably fallen in love.

Hell, maybe he should have begged.

13

ALONE IN HIS OFFICE around 4:00 a.m., Joe finally cracked his computer program. It simply clicked into place. Once upon a time, he would have jumped up and down, shouting and whooping for joy.

Now the victory was hollow and meaningless.

Yes, he'd been working for the better part of three years on the office system he knew would redefine software as most knew it. And yes, he'd once measured his success by it.

Success meant nothing now. Nothing at all without Caitlin to share it with.

Swiping his hands down over his haggard face, he looked around at the darkened office. The only light came from the glow of his computer. The only sound was from the coffeemaker down the hall—which was running perfectly smoothly now that the wiring had been fixed.

Still, what he wouldn't give for Caitlin to be here blowing it up at this very moment.

Because only then would everything be perfect.

He'd once harbored great dreams on this program. It would make him famous. Make him a somebody. Give him wealth and security for the rest of his life.

Now he didn't care about any of that. All he wanted was to be a somebody to a beautiful, caring woman named Caitlin Taylor, who wanted nothing to do with a cold jerk like himself.

He couldn't blame her.

Shoving back from his desk, he stalked toward the door, suddenly needed fresh air.

Once outside, he stepped around the sleeping homeless man on the stoop and watched the early morning. Tipping his head back, he studied the stars.

A cool breeze rumpled his hair. In the distance, he could hear the drone of the cars on the freeway, and knew he'd get better scenery at home on the beach, where he could feel the cool ocean spray and smell the salt on the wind.

But at home, he'd be reminded of his failures. He'd probably stand in his bedroom and fantasize about having Caitlin back in his bed, golden hair spread on his pillow, her dark eyes wide with sensual wonder. Just thinking about it brought back the scent of her, the satiny feel of her skin against his.

If he closed his eyes, it was so clear in his mind. The huge bed. Sighs and murmurs, the whisper of clothing floating to the floor. The gentle, full spring wind teasing the curtains and blowing the air over their heated skin...

He'd driven her away, and the way he saw it now, he had two choices. He could be a complete fool and live, suffer with his decision to keep his love to himself.

Or he could do what he'd sworn never to do— beg.

HE'D SEARCHED the entire world for her. At least it felt that way. With humbling defeat, Joe tossed his keys aside, plopped down in his chair and set his head on the desk.

It was late afternoon, and he had to face the devastating facts.

Caitlin had disappeared.

"Still no luck, Joe?" Andy asked from the doorway.

Joe didn't lift his head, but knew Tim would be hovering there, as well, waiting for news. "Nope."

"You looked in her condo?"

Only six times. "Yep."

"And you checked your place again, right?" This from Tim, sounding worried.

Worried was a good thing, Joe decided, because if either Andy or Tim was hiding her, he would have to kill them. "Yes, I checked my place again." He'd left it unlocked, actually, hoping against hope. But she hadn't shown.

"Did her father have a place?"

"It's been sold, but yes, I checked there, too. And the hotels and motels in the area." And the hospitals, the police station, and out of sheer desperation, three of the closest shopping malls. He'd even driven to Amy's apartment, after he'd begged the landlord for her address. No one had answered.

Caitlin had vanished, and he'd never in his life been so sick or guilt-ridden.

"So you screwed up already, huh?"

Vince. He'd been suspiciously absent earlier this morning. Joe surged to his feet, rage ready. "Tell me where she is."

Vince shot him a half smile. "Flattering that you think she'd come to me." His smile faded to disgust. "All you had to do was love her, Joe. She's like the most perfect woman ever made. What was so hard about giving her your all?"

"Tell me, damn you."

Both Tim and Andy wisely slunk back, out of sight.

Vince just shrugged. "I don't know any more than you do where she is, but I'll tell you this. If I find her first, you won't stand a chance in hell."

Joe searched his face for any sign of deception and found none. He sank back to his chair in defeat. "You really don't know where she is, do you?"

Stuffing his hands into his trouser pockets, Vince leaned back against the wall and shook his head. "Do you think she's all right?"

Joe's anger abruptly drained. "God, I hope so." Shoving his fingers through his hair, he leaped up again, unable to sit still. He started pacing. "I'm the biggest idiot on earth."

"Nah." Vince managed a grin. "Well, maybe. But at least you're the richest one. I can't believe how much they're going to pay for that system, Joe. Not to mention the royalties. I just can't believe it."

"All we have is a very small, preliminary commitment from one phone call. They still have to test it, prove to themselves it does what I say it does," Joe warned soberly. "I hope you're not disappointed I decided to sell it rather than market it ourselves."

"Are you kidding? If it works out, you just set me and the twins up for life." Vince's joy faded. "But how about you? Are you set up for life, as well?"

Joe looked out the window. Below, the city was flowing smoothly into evening traffic. The streets were crawling with commuters, seething with activity. He sighed. "Not until I find Caitlin."

TWO DAYS LATER, Joe was out of his mind with torment. How could Caitlin have just disappeared into thin air?

It amazed him, the turn everything had taken. In just two short days, he'd gotten a request for a complete new system, one that would keep him busy for a long time to come. This, on top of a bid for the system he'd just completed. They'd offered about five times what he'd expected, which should have been the thrill of a lifetime. If Edmund were alive, he'd be cackling over the fact that suddenly Joe had more money than he.

But Edmund wasn't alive, Caitlin was gone and the victory meant nothing.

His phone rang and he leaped at it, heart pounding. "Yes?" he barked, hope cruelly flaring.

"Joe, could you come up here?"

Darla. Hope deflated, leaving despair. "I'm busy."

"You always say that."

"I can't face the tax stuff right now, Darla," he said quietly. Outside his window, two flights down, a young woman walked, holding a toddler's hand. The little girl, awed by the size of the buildings around her, craned her head upward and seemed to stare right into Joseph's eyes.

God, I want one of those, he thought as his heart constricted. *I want a family, and I want it with Caitlin.*

"Please come, Joe," Darla said into his ear, her voice no longer friendly, but urgent. "You won't be sorry."

He stared at the receiver after she hung up. Darla never asked him for anything unless it was absolutely necessary. So it was with a sigh that he left his office and headed toward the elevator.

When he entered Darla's suite minutes later, she rushed out of one of her offices and yanked him into another before he could draw a breath.

"What the—"

"Shush." Darla locked the door and shoved him into a chair.

"Darla," he said slowly, carefully, straightening. "This is flattering, but—"

"Shut up, Brownley." Darla slapped her hands on her slim hips and glared at him. "I can't believe how slow you are." She paced the room. "I promised not to get involved and normally I'm pretty good at promises, but I'm reneging on this one. It's going to cause problems, but I think maybe it's worth it."

He was getting dizzy watching her pace. "What the hell are you talking about?"

"I haven't got the details figured out yet. She's much, much smarter than I gave her credit for, but I think if you—"

Joe went still. "Darla."

"It should work. I think if you really play it up right, she'll feel so sorry for you, she'll *have* to give in. For some reason, she's a sucker for you, which does work in your favor."

It was difficult, very difficult, to remain calm with his heart blocking his windpipe. "You know where Caitlin is."

Darla stopped pacing and looked at him as if he were an idiot. "Of course I do."

Slowly, in order to not kill her before she gave him the information he needed, he advanced on her. "Tell me where she is. Afterward, you can tell me why you kept it from me for nearly three days when you knew how much this meant to me."

Darla's eyes went soft with regret, but she kept the presence of mind to back up. "I'm sorry, Joe. But she was so hurt, and you really messed things up. She begged me to keep quiet, but now, after watching her work while trying not to mourn over you, I think I did the wrong thing by promising not to tell you. I think she really loves you. And I know you love her too, way deep down in that black heart of yours."

He came closer, and her words came faster. "So could you do me a favor, a really big one?" She rushed her words. "Could you go out there and make my new full-charge bookkeeper-in-training smile? Could you turn her grief into joy so that I can get some real work done?"

That stopped him short. "You hired Caitlin?"

"Well, you've seen what she can do with numbers. Besides, I like her." Her face softened. "A lot."

"But—"

"You should see the mind that lurks behind that ridiculous come-hither haircut...my God, Joe. She loves numbers almost as much as I do. She can't answer the phones too well, and she tends to distract my male clients all to hell, but you should see her reconcile a checkbook. A girl after my own heart."

He was jerking the door open, nerves and hope singing through his veins. "You can't keep her—she's mine."

"Wanna make a bet?"

When he growled, she laughed. "Let the best boss win," she said diplomatically.

She smiled when he slammed out. "I'm such a hopeless romantic," she whispered, and sank into her chair to get some work done.

IT WAS LATE AFTERNOON by the time Caitlin finished sorting out the bank account of one of Darla's clients. It had been a mess of mismatched checks, wrong deposits and untotaled columns. At first, she'd panicked, but after looking closer, she'd gotten excited.

It *was* a mess, but it was just a matter of shopping around for the right numbers—and no one understood shopping better than Caitlin Taylor. Besides, somehow, the mess appealed. Maybe because she so understood the misguided logic that had created the disaster in the first place. Maybe because she loved to sort and add and organize. Maybe just because she felt thrilled about feeling so useful. So purposeful.

It should have made her very happy. It shouldn't have had her gaze covered in a sheen of unshed tears.

"No," she muttered, blinking them ruthlessly back as she stuck her pencil into the electric sharpener. "I won't cry another tear for him. Not one."

"I don't blame you."

She nearly started right out of her chair at the sound of that familiar, unbearably sexy voice behind her.

"Hi," he said softly when she looked up at him. Slowly, he shut her office door. He walked over to her desk while her heart raced. He looked the same. Stone-washed faded jeans fitted to that long, lean, mouth-watering body. Simple white T-shirt stretched across his chest. Brown wavy hair falling over his forehead, as wayward as the owner. But it was his eyes, those light blue, all-seeing eyes, that stopped her heart.

They held her, caressed her, refused to let her go.

"Are you going to sharpen that pencil until it's gone?"

With a soft oath, she jerked it out of the sharpener. "What are you doing here?"

He smiled at her, then took a little bow. "Your new secretary at your service, ma'am."

14

CAITLIN COULD ONLY STARE at him. "I'm sorry. I don't understand."

Joe leaned a hip against her desk, propping his weight against it. "It's simple. You're so busy working the accounts, Darla hired me to…answer phones for you. And…" His gaze searched the room, and she wasn't so far gone in her own misery that she missed the nerves and tension in his eyes.

"And?" she prompted, uncertain.

He lifted a shoulder. "And whatever else you need."

"What if I don't need anything?"

Now he looked desperate, as well as stressed. "I can make coffee," he added, brightening. "Real good coffee."

She let out a little disbelieving laugh, but had no idea what to say. Her fingers fiddled on her desk for something to do. Grabbing another pencil, she shoved it into the sharpener.

"Are you going to sharpen all your pencils now?" he asked conversationally. "Because I could do that for you."

"I don't need any help from you."

"I understand." His gruff voice clearly said

the opposite. So did his hungry gaze as it swept over her. "I certainly brushed *you* off enough times, didn't I?"

"Is that what this is about?"

"Partly." He gave her a little smile. "You have no idea how good it is to see you, Caitlin."

"I've...been busy."

Undeterred, he slid closer, and his gaze was the most soul-shaking, heart-wrenching one she'd ever seen. "You scared me to death, you know," he said quietly. "I'm not sure whether to throttle you or kiss you silly."

Unable to sit and calmly talk after all that had transpired between them, she surged to her feet. With lithe grace, he rose, as well, and they ended up toe-to-toe...face-to-face.

"Neither appeals," she said quickly.

He touched her cheek gently, tenderly. "Why don't we kiss and make sure."

It took every ounce of self-control she had not to throw herself at him. "There's nothing left, Joe."

"I'm sorry you feel that way."

"No," she said, her eyes stinging. He'd not stopped touching her in that way he had, the way that told her how much he cared. "That's how *you* feel."

"You're wrong. There's our future, for one thing."

She might have scoffed, except he was looking at her as though willing her to understand. She didn't. "We have no future, Joe. The things I said—about loving you. I was mistaken." She met his gaze and wasn't at all satisfied to see the pain her words had caused. She faltered, and knew if he didn't leave now, she'd crumple. "Please go."

The phone rang, and before she could reach for it, Joe smoothly scooped it up. "Ms. Taylor's desk... No, I'm sorry. She's unavailable at this time. A problem with your account?" He listened seriously. "I see. Okay. Hold on, I'll get her." Without taking his eyes off her, he hung up the phone.

She gaped at him. "Are you crazy? That's not how to put someone on hold."

"Oops," he said mildly. "Sorry. Would you like to talk now?"

She let out a baffled laugh. "Do I have a choice?" She wished he didn't look so good. Wished she didn't miss him so much that she was shaking with it.

He looked at her bleakly, all cockiness and self-assurance gone. "Where have you been, Caitlin? Have you had a place to stay? Enough money to get by? Dammit, are you even eating?"

"God, don't." She made herself busy at the shelving unit against the wall. "Don't talk to me in that voice. It makes me hurt."

He followed her, his big body sheltering her with warmth. "I hate it that you hurt. I hate that I caused it."

"Please," she begged him, unwilling to break

down in front of him. "Please, just go. I can't handle this—"

"If you'd just listen for a minute—"

"I *have* listened to you! All my life, I've been listening to someone, blindly following. Well, I'm through with all that!" She was shouting now and she didn't care. "I'm listening to myself for a change!"

He held her close when she started to shake with anger, but then her anger was gone and it was grief making her tremble. "I'm listening to myself."

"The way I should have all along."

It was the steely quiet in his tone that made her look at him. "What do you mean?"

His hands gentled on her, but he didn't let go. "I'm sorrier than I can say, Caitlin. You tried to tell me so many things—how you needed more to do on the job, that your father had pretty much deserted you...the way you felt about me. I didn't listen," he said with disgust aimed at himself, "because I couldn't handle how you made me feel."

"And how did I make you feel?"

"Terrified," he said without hesitation. "Caitlin, I know next to nothing about letting people close to me. Even less about families and love. I was never close to anyone until your father. I taught myself to hold back, to protect myself, because it was easier. I couldn't get hurt that way."

"That's no way to live," she told him huskily. "*I* can't live that way."

His smile was warm and completely unexpected. "I know. You throw yourself whole-heartedly into absolutely everything you do. You give it your all, one hundred percent of the time, not worrying first about whether you're going to get hurt or not. It's one of the things I love most about you."

Afraid to read too much into his words, she crossed her arms over her chest and backed up a step, out of his reach so he couldn't touch her. So she couldn't touch him.

"I cared when I didn't want to," he said. "I worried when I swore I wouldn't. And, dammit," he said roughly, his voice breaking, "I really need you to break in any time here and tell me you meant it when you told me you loved me."

Tears filled her eyes as she stared at him mute. Panic filled him. "Wait!" he said quickly, slapping his forehead as he remembered. "Wait a minute. I have to tell you first. God, I really stink at this." He drew a deep, ragged breath and met her drenched eyes. "I fell in love with you, Caitlin. No matter how many times I told myself I couldn't, that I wouldn't, I did." Lifting her hand to his lips, he kissed her knuckles. "I love you hopelessly. Will you stay with me forever? Be my wife?"

She looked at him for an eternal moment, for once her eyes shuttering her thoughts from him.

"I don't want to go back to work for you," she said finally.

What did that mean? he wondered wildly. But then, beyond the tears, he saw the teasing light in her expression. Relief, joy and a thousand other surging emotions rushed through him.

"No offense," she told him teasingly as a tear slipped down her cheek, "but Darla pays better. Much better."

"I'll triple your salary," he said without skipping a beat, cupping her face and swiping another tear away with the pad of his thumb. "Quadruple."

She tilted her head as she considered. "I get to do your accounting. All of it."

"Okay, but I'll make the coffee," he said quickly, flashing a sudden grin as his heart threatened to burst. "Caitlin. Tell me. Tell me you love me quick, that you forgive me for being such a fool. I'm dying here."

She smiled, a brilliant radiance spreading across her features. "I forgive you for being a fool. And I love you with all my heart."

"Thank God," he murmured, yanking her against him. He kissed her, his mouth open and warm, receiving and giving, full of enough promises to last a lifetime.

Lifting her head, she looked up at him, taking a moment to bask in the joy of their love. "Let's talk benefits."

Eyes dancing with love and laughter, he

pulled her close. "Anything you want, Mrs. Brownley-to-be. Anything you want."

"Well, there's just a couple of little things...." She pulled him close and whispered her heart's wishes.

He made them all come true.

Epilogue

THE LETTER CAME one week after their wedding. Caitlin stared at her father's familiar handwriting and her pounding heart landed in her throat.

"What's the matter?" Joe came up behind her, slipped his arms around her waist. Leaning over her shoulder, he frowned. "That's Edmund's writing. How—?" His arms tightened on her in reaction. "Where did that come from?"

"The mail." She patted his hand, knowing the gruffness in his voice was grief. "My father's attorney sent it to me." Quickly, with fingers that shook, Caitlin ripped open the envelope.

As she read, her heart warmed, tightening in her chest until she thought she might burst with love and happiness. She whirled to face Joe, her eyes burning, her throat thick. In his gaze, she saw equal emotion, and knew he'd already read the note. "He loved me," she whispered.

"Very much," Joe whispered back, bending to kiss her softly. "So much that he hid away a trust fund for you. He just wanted to be sure you'd be okay without him. Without his money."

"It says here that he always knew I was smart, tough—" Her voice cracked a little. "But he wanted *me* to know it, too." She smiled through a haze of tears. "He'd have loved that we found each other. He was so proud of you."

Joe cupped her face and looked down at her with love swimming in his eyes. "He'd be so proud of you, too."

Caitlin sighed. "I can't imagine what we're going to do with all that money."

"No?" Joe smiled. "A year ago, you wouldn't have given it a second thought."

"I'd have shopped until I dropped." She smiled. "Joe, how do you feel about setting up a charity for women who've been dumped on?"

"You mean divorced?"

"Yeah. Or deserted in any way at all." She grinned. This was the delicious part. "We could train them to make it on their own. Teach them important skills." She tucked her tongue firmly in her cheek and gazed up at Joe with adoring affection. "You know, such as respect for their employer, making coffee, or...how to pick the proper business attire."

He gave a shout of laughter and hugged her close.

Suddenly serious, she leaned back. "I want to do this, Joe. We can train them in bookkeeping. *Anything*. Just so that they don't feel worthless or helpless. What do you think?"

His breath caught because she could still dazzle him with just a look. "I think I've never been more proud, or loved you so much, Caitlin Taylor Brownley." He bent to give her another kiss, his love, his life.

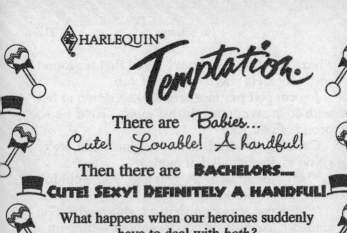

If you enjoyed what you just read,
then we've got an offer you can't resist!

Take 2 bestselling love stories FREE!

Plus get a FREE surprise gift!

Clip this page and mail it to Harlequin Reader Service®

IN U.S.A.	IN CANADA
3010 Walden Ave.	P.O. Box 609
P.O. Box 1867	Fort Erie, Ontario
Buffalo, N.Y. 14240-1867	L2A 5X3

YES! Please send me 2 free Harlequin Temptation® novels and my free surprise gift. Then send me 4 brand-new novels every month, which I will receive months before they're available in stores. In the U.S.A., bill me at the bargain price of $3.12 plus 25¢ delivery per book and applicable sales tax, if any*. In Canada, bill me at the bargain price of $3.57 plus 25¢ delivery per book and applicable taxes**. That's the complete price and a savings of over 10% off the cover prices—what a great deal! I understand that accepting the 2 free books and gift places me under no obligation ever to buy any books. I can always return a shipment and cancel at any time. Even if I never buy another book from Harlequin, the 2 free books and gift are mine to keep forever. So why not take us up on our invitation. You'll be glad you did!

142 HEN CNEV
342 HEN CNEW

Name	(PLEASE PRINT)	
Address	Apt.#	
City	State/Prov.	Zip/Postal Code

* Terms and prices subject to change without notice. Sales tax applicable in N.Y.
** Canadian residents will be charged applicable provincial taxes and GST.
All orders subject to approval. Offer limited to one per household.
® are registered trademarks of Harlequin Enterprises Limited.

TEMP99   ©1998 Harlequin Enterprises Limited

"Fascinating—you'll want to take this home!"
—Marie Ferrarella

"Each page is filled with a brand-new surprise."
—Suzanne Brockmann

"Makes reading a new and joyous experience all over again."
—Tara Taylor Quinn

See what all your favorite authors are talking about.

Coming October 1999 to a retail store near you.

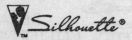

In celebration of Harlequin®'s golden anniversary

Enter to win a *dream!* You could win:

- A luxurious trip for two to *The Renaissance Cottonwoods Resort* in Scottsdale, Arizona, or

- A bouquet of flowers once a week for a year from **FTD**, or

- A $500 shopping spree, or

- A fabulous bath & body gift basket, including **K-tel**'s *Candlelight and Romance* 5-CD set.

Look for **WIN A DREAM** flash on specially marked Harlequin® titles by Penny Jordan, Dallas Schulze, Anne Stuart and Kristine Rolofson in October 1999*.

RENAISSANCE.
COTTONWOODS RESORT
SCOTTSDALE, ARIZONA

K-TEL

COMING NEXT MONTH

#745 BABY.COM Molly Liholm
Bachelors & Babies

When bachelor Sam Evans finds a baby on his doorstep he's surprised. Little Juliette even comes with a web page and care instructions! *Then* Anne Logan appears on Sam's doorstep. The sexy nanny agrees to help, but soon she doesn't know *who* is more trouble—the teething tot or lovesick Sam!

#746 A CLASS ACT Pamela Burford
15th Anniversary Celebration!

Voted "Most Likely To...Succeed," lawyer Gabe Moreau has done exactly that. But he's never forgotten gorgeous Dena Devlin. Time hasn't erased the hurt...or the hot sizzling attraction between them. Their high school reunion will be the perfect place to reignite those feelings....

#747 NIGHT WHISPERS Leslie Kelly

DJ Kelsey Logan knows what she wants—stuffy but sexy Mitch Wymore. So what if the handsome prof doesn't care for her late-night radio venue "Night Whispers"! It's a show about romance and fantasy—two things Kelsey is absolutely convinced Mitch needs in his life....

#748 THE SEDUCTION OF SYDNEY Jamie Denton
Blaze

Sydney Travers's biological clock is ticking loudly, but there's no suitable daddy in sight. Except Derek Buchanan, who is her best friend and *hardly* lover material. But Sydney has no idea the sexy scientist is in love with her—and determined to seduce Sydney at the first opportunity.